THE BILLIONAIRE'S FORBIDDEN DESIRES

A Second Chance Baby Romance (Irresistible Brothers Prequel)

SCARLETT KING

MICHELLE LOVE

CONTENTS

Blurb   v

1. Coy   1
2. Collin   6
3. Fiona   13
4. Collin   19
5. Coy   26
6. Fiona   31
7. Collin   36
8. Fiona   41
9. Collin   48
10. Lila   55
11. Fiona   62
12. Collin   70
13. Fiona   76
14. Collin   81
15. Fiona   89
16. Coy   95
17. Lila   102
18. Coy   108
19. Lila   114
20. Coy   121
21. Lila   127
22. Coy   134
23. Lila   141
24. Coy   147
25. Lila   153
    Epilogue   161

    Collin   163
    Lila   167

Published in the USA by Scarlett King & Michelle Love

©Copyright 2021

ISBN-13: 9781648089985

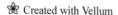 Created with Vellum

BLURB

I've bent her near to the breaking point for
what she's stolen from me—my heart.
But she will never carry my name.
Only a woman of integrity can have that
— only integrity isn't my cup of tea.
It's time to grow up and be responsible.
Leave the past where it belongs.
Leave my sinful ways behind and find a good woman.
A woman that my family will accept.
She'll have to stay with me—in secret—feeding my darkest
desires.

COY

May 1988 – Carthage, Texas

My high school graduation party, meant to reacquaint me with those I'd attended kindergarten with, had me nearly as nervous as the day my parents dropped me off at boarding school in Dallas when I was just six years old. "This is surreal."

My mother patted me on the back as she smiled. "I know it feels that way to you. I want you to have a good time, though. So, don't let nerves get the best of you, son."

Nodding, I sipped on some punch as people began showing up. At first, I stayed seated, but then I got up and went to the door to welcome everyone and introduce myself to those I'd known back when I was young. "Coy Gentry." I shook a guy's hand as he came in.

"Yeah, I know." Freckles speckled his face as he smiled at me. "Tanner Richardson — I sat behind you in our kindergarten class."

"Wow, you remember that?" I couldn't believe it. "It's great to see you again, Tanner."

"Yeah, you too, Coy."

I pointed to the refreshments. "Go grab something to eat and drink, and we'll catch up later on."

As soon as he walked away, another guy I recognized from school entered, and then more and more of my old classmates followed. In no time, I felt as comfortable as I'd felt at boarding school with the kids I'd grown up with.

Chatting with a group of guys as we hung out on the outer edge of the dancefloor, the band playing a slow country song, I caught something out of the corner of my eye. When I turned to see what had captured my attention, I was left breathless.

She had long, dark hair that shone in the twinkling lights. Her dark eyes reminded me of those of a doe's, and her caramel complexion, flawless. My eyes moved down her body, finding curves that some might find to be on the dangerous side — I found them delightful.

Scanning back up her body, I realized that her eyes were on mine and that a smile was curving her plump lips. I moved toward her, pulled in like a magnet. "Wanna dance?"

"Okay." She held her hand out, and I took it.

For a moment, I had no idea what was happening. My head felt light, my heart sped up as sparks of electricity shot all through me, and my manhood tingled. "Thanks."

Pulling her into my arms, making sure to leave some respectful distance between our bodies, I began to move slowly back and forth. "So, your name is?"

"Oh, yeah. I forgot to introduce myself. I'm Coy Gentry. And you are?"

"Lila Stevens." Pink filled her cheeks as her eyes darted away from mine. "So, I'm dancing with the guy who's throwing this party."

"You are." I pulled her a bit closer, inhaling her scent. Baby powder and the slightest hint of lemons made me heady for some reason. "Did you graduate this year too?"

"I did. I wasn't in your kindergarten class, though. But the ad in the newspaper said this party was for the entire graduating class of Carthage High." Her hand moved across my shoulder as she got more comfortable in my arms. "I heard you went to an all-boys school. So, where'd you learn how to dance?"

"We had socials with all-girls schools." I liked the way she moved. "You dance well. Where'd you learn how to dance?"

"At local dances. So, I guess you'll be leaving to go to college at the end of the summer."

"Yeah. Lubbock to Texas Tech. That's where both my parents went."

"Your mom was my third-grade teacher. She talked about you, and there were pictures of you on her desk too. You were a cute kid." She ducked her head as if feeling shy. "You've grown into a handsome young man, Coy Gentry."

My body heated. "You're a beautiful young woman, Lila Stevens."

"I bet you say that to all girls." She laughed a little. I loved the way it sounded.

"I do not." I hadn't dated anyone. My studies were too important to let romance interfere. At least, that's what my father and grandfather had shoved down my throat since I'd hit puberty. "I haven't talked to many girls."

Her dark eyes widened. "So, am I to believe that I'm the first girl you've called beautiful?"

It was the truth. "You are."

The band switched to another song, this one on the faster side, so we had to move around the dancefloor, dancing the Texas two-step. With the music loud and the movement fast, we didn't talk; we just danced and laughed.

This is nice.

I couldn't seem to let her go, and before I knew it, we'd danced until we were out of breath. I didn't let go of her hand as I led her off the dancefloor. "Come on, let's get a drink."

"I'm with ya, Coy. Whew! You can sure tear up a dancefloor."

"So can you." I picked up a cup that was already filled with fruit punch and handed it to her. "Here ya go."

After we took a few gulps of the cold beverage, she asked, "When do you have to take off to Lubbock?"

"At the end of the summer. Are you heading out to college then too?"

"No. I'd go if I could. My family doesn't have the money to send any of us to school. It's just the way it is. I'll probably get a job at the grocery store or something like that. You can work your way up there. Start out sacking groceries, move up to cashier, then up to head cashier, and maybe even assistant manager a few years later."

She looked smarter than that. "Well, I bet you move up to a manager in no time, Lila."

Laughter peeled through the air as she must've thought it to be a crazy notion. "You've got faith in me that my family doesn't."

I didn't like to hear that. "I'm not trying to pry, but how were your grades in school?"

"A's and B's. I'm not dumb. It's complicated, but my family kind of keeps us all grounded, and we tend to stay in the same lane they walked in. Do you know what I mean?" She sipped the punch, then licked the red off of her lips.

A tremble ran through me as I watched her tongue graze over her lips. "Uh, yeah." I'd lost my train of thought as my manhood stirred. "Are you doing anything tomorrow?"

"Depends." Placing one hand on her hip, she cocked her head to one side.

"Depends on what?"

"What you're about to ask me to do with you."

"I thought I might take you up to Dallas and show you where I went to school, and then I'd take you to this fancy restaurant that's shaped like a huge sphere and is way up in the sky. It turns around in slow circles so you can see the entire downtown skyline too. Some of us went this one time, and I thought it would be the perfect place to take a date."

4

"How many dates have you taken there?"

I didn't want her to know how inexperienced I was. But then again, I didn't want to lie either. "Lila, I feel like I can be honest with you, and you won't make fun of me."

Her eyes drooped a little as she put the drink down and took my hand. "I promise you that I won't."

Relief spread through me. "Well, Lila, you're the first girl I've asked out."

Blinking a few times, she asked, "Are you serious right now?"

"I am." Butterflies began to swarm inside my stomach as I anticipated her walking away from me.

"Wow." She smiled and squeezed my hand. "What an honor. I would love to go on a date with you tomorrow, Coy."

"So, that's a yes, then?" I had to ask to be sure there wasn't a but that was still coming.

"That is a yes."

I've got a feeling this is going to turn out great!

COLLIN

September 1966 – Lubbock, Texas

"Guns up!" I held my hands up, pointing my finger to the sky, just like the rest of the people in the crowded stadium as the Red Riders took the football field. My last year at Texas Tech University would be one to remember, I'd make damn sure of that.

One year away from earning a bachelor's degree in Agriculture, I was well on my way to making my father proud. That was the mission—make Daddy proud.

My father was very exacting—he demanded certain things of me. And if I failed him, I got my ass handed to me. He'd taught me to be tough and unrelenting in anything I did. And so far, it had paid off.

I'd made good grades and got my name on the Dean's list. That had earned me a nice new truck from my father. When I went back home at the end of the school year and handed him my diploma, I knew I'd earn even more.

Managing the ranch my grandfather had built was my ultimate goal. My father would finally show me how everything worked. I'd been taught how to take care of the cattle, but I hadn't been taught the business part of the ranch. I was eager to get to that.

During the summer break, my parents had spoken a lot about my future—about how it was time for me to find a good woman from a good family and settle down.

There was a girl back home who'd taken my heart. But she wasn't marriage material in my father's eyes. She came from the wrong side of town. Her family was poor, and her father a drunk. Not the kind of people my father wanted attached to the Gentry family name.

It wasn't easy to find the right woman to marry when I still had that girl on my mind. But I knew I had to get on the ball, or my father would be disappointed. And when Daddy was disappointed, things got really hard for me.

"Excuse me, please," a feminine voice spoke up beside me, making me look away from the football game. She moved to the seat on my other side, a smile on her pretty face. She had a creamy ivory complexion, bright blue eyes, and blonde hair pulled back into a high ponytail. "Don't worry, I won't bother you by asking lots of questions about the game. Even though I don't understand it at all." She smoothed out her denim skirt, running her hands along her bottom to tuck it under before sitting down.

A white, button-down shirt, starched and ironed, was tucked into the waistline of a skirt that fell down past her knees, even when she sat down. She looked the part of a college girl. She looked the part of a nice girl from a nice family.

I didn't say anything to her, though, just gave her a nod, then looked back to the football field. A breeze blew past her, sending a fresh scent to my nose. She smelled nice too. A nice girl from a nice family, who smelled nice.

"I haven't seen you around here before." I looked at her for only a moments and then quickly looked back at the field.

"I've just transferred here. I've been going to the University of Texas in Austin. But my father's company moved him to the Lubbock office. My parents haven't allowed me to live on campus, so I had to come with them up here. Daddy told me to go to a football game, so I could get to know people."

I hadn't asked for her life story. But I wasn't going to say that to her. "I'm Collin Gentry, from Carthage."

"Oh, how silly of me." She held out her hand as if she wanted to shake mine.

I looked at her hand, then took it, shaking it. "Why's that?"

"I haven't told you *my* name yet," she said as she laughed a little. "I'm Fiona Walton, currently from Lubbock, formerly from Austin. Isn't Carthage around the Dallas area?"

"It's about two and a half hours from Dallas, but it's the nearest big city. We've got a ranch. That's why I'm going to school here. I'm getting a bachelor's in ag."

"Well, that makes perfect sense if you're a rancher. I'm getting a bachelor's in education so I can become a teacher."

She looked like someone who'd become a teacher. And teaching was a noble profession. "I think you'd make an excellent teacher."

"Thank you. I think I will too. I adore children." She ran her hand over her ponytail. The sunlight made the golden strands sparkle.

"I've never been around children to know if I like them or not."

She laughed, and the sound made me smile. "You're funny."

I wasn't trying to be funny. But I liked her laugh. "Am I?"

A kid came into the stands with a box hanging around his neck filled with sodas, popcorn, and hotdogs. I held up two fingers, and he came my way. "What can I get ya, mister?"

"Two dogs, a bag of that popcorn, and a couple of sodas." I took the first soda he handed me and gave it to Fiona.

"Oh, for me?" She took the drink as she smiled. "Well, thank you, Collin Gentry."

I handed her one of the hotdogs too, and then put the popcorn bag in her lap. "Don't mention it, Fiona."

Biting into the warm hotdog, I realized I liked the way I felt with her. It was an easy feeling. We sat there, watching the game and eating without saying a word for a long time. And that was okay.

Our team was losing pretty badly when the quarterback caught the ball and ran for a touchdown. Everyone stood up, cheering him on—even Fiona. "Go, go, go!"

For a girl who didn't understand the game, she'd caught on quickly. When our team scored the touchdown, the crowd went wild. There was no way they could win the game, but at least now there would be a number on the scoreboard instead of a big fat goose egg.

As we sat back down, I opened my mouth, and out came words I hadn't thought of saying. "Wanna go get a chocolate malt and some fries when this is over?"

"Sure." Her cheeks went a nice shade of pink. "That sounds yummy."

"There's this little hole-in-the-wall café. It's got good cheeseburgers too. If you're hungry."

"I'm sure I will be by the time the game is over." The stadium lights came on as the sun had almost set, making her blue eyes sparkle.

Mom would like her.

Seeing as I wasn't into wasting my time on any woman, I had a few things I had to know about Fiona before I went any further. "You goin' to church in the morning?"

"With my family, yes." She winked at me. "The First Baptist Church downtown."

She's passed the religion test.

"That's nice."

"Will you be there?" she asked.

"Me?" I didn't go to church unless my parents made me.

"Yes, you."

"Well, no."

9

"I see."

On to the next one. It wasn't easy to ask a question about one's political choice, so coming up with that wasn't easy. After a few minutes of thinking hard about it, I finally said, "So, a Texan in the White House."

Her eyes cut to me as her lips pulled up to one side. "You're referring to President Lyndon B. Johnson?"

"Yes." I didn't exactly know how to say it, but knew I had to figure that out. "What do you think about him?"

"I think he's done a wonderful job. I voted for him over Barry Goldwater in the sixty-four election."

Another correct answer.

She was nearing a perfect score. "You said you moved here because of your father's job. What does he do?"

"My father's an investment banker."

Score!

"Good job."

"It is a pretty good job." She smiled at me as her eyes twinkled. "You're a rancher, which is a good job as well. How'd you vote in the last election?"

"For the man who won." I knew she was onto me. I grinned at her. "And I'm a Baptist too. Christmas and Easter, I take the back pew while Momma and Daddy take their seats up front, as usual."

"Yes, my family likes to sit up front too. I sit with them." She looked at me for a long moment as I kept staring straight ahead. "It would be nice to see you in church tomorrow, Collin. I'll save you a seat right next to me—just in case you decide to come."

She seemed to be checking off boxes the same way I was. I knew if I didn't go to church the next day, she'd never give me the time of day again. If I went to church, she'd probably give me all the attention I could handle.

"Who knows, you might just see me there, sittin' next to you tomorrow morning. I assume services start at ten and end around noon? We could get lunch afterward."

"My mother always puts a roast on before we leave for church. So, you could come to our home for lunch."

We were setting up dates left and right. And, for once, no one would be angry or upset with me over who I was dating. For once, I could take my girl out in public without fear of my father finding out and tanning my hide. For once, I wouldn't have to hide my relationship. "It's been a while since I had a good home-cooked meal."

"My mother is a wonderful cook. I'm not too bad myself either."

And she can cook too?

"I bet you are. What'll you be making for tomorrow's lunch?"

"I think I'll make some black-eyed peas and a pan of cornbread."

I have hit the jackpot!

But there was one thing I had to know first. "Do you add sugar to your cornbread?"

"Never."

And we have a winner!

"Good. I hate when people make the cornbread sweet. It makes it taste like cake, and who wants to have cake with their meal? Not me."

"I hope you like sweet tea. Mom always makes that. She serves it over plenty of ice, too."

This girl is almost too good to be true.

"What's a meal without ice-cold sweet tea?"

"I know." She laughed again.

I couldn't help but smile at her. She was perfect. She'd make any man proud to call her his.

My father would be proud if I brought this little filly home to the ranch. Momma would adore her too. And me—well, I would like her. She was nice. Pretty. Wholesome.

Those weren't things I particularly looked for in a woman. I usually liked a bit more excitement—some darkness instead of pure-white purity. But my father wouldn't allow that. So, I would give him what he wanted. And I could be happy enough with a woman like Fiona.

Happy enough was better than nothing. Happy enough was something I could build a life around.

Maybe I wasn't meant to have it all. Maybe no one was. But I could have a nice life with this nice girl. We'd have some nice-looking kids, too. Kids that our families would accept.

The girl I had left behind had given up so much for me, and here I was, looking at this pretty young woman with thoughts of marriage and raising a family with her. Guilt wasn't a thing I often felt, but as I thought about how hurt she'd be when I went back to Carthage with a wife, guilt welled up inside of me.

My father's voice echoed in my brain, "Time to grow up and do the responsible adult thing, Collin. Leave the past where it belongs. Leave your sinful ways behind you, and go into the future with a good woman. A woman the whole family will proudly call a Gentry."

I can do wholesome—I think. df

3

FIONA

Collin Gentry wasn't the most polite man, nor was he the most talkative. He was very handsome, though, and that made up for the things he lacked.

I blamed it on him being raised on a ranch with cattle and other animals instead of plenty of people. It was clear that he liked his solitude, never staying out past ten on none of the nights we had a date. He'd tell me that he had to get back to his dorm so he could wind down before going to sleep.

I'd had a couple of boyfriends before. They'd both had a hard time leaving me after they'd taken me out. Collin had no trouble leaving me at all.

We'd been dating for three months, and he'd never done more than kiss my cheek. He rarely held my hand, and he never told me how pretty I was or how happy I made him feel.

Somehow, I knew he did like me, though. He kept making time to see me—that let me know that I was special to him. Collin didn't care to spend time with anyone other than me. That had to mean something.

He'd met my parents, of course, as he joined us for lunch after church every Sunday. That was another reason I knew that he liked me. He'd come to church each Sunday since we'd met, sitting next to me in the front row, despite what he'd said when we'd first talked at the football game. No man would do a thing like that unless they actually liked a woman.

I'd never known a guy like Collin. Quiet, not in a rush to get to the first kiss or second or third base. My father told me he suspected Collin was looking at me as wife material. And he'd asked me what I thought about that, should the time come that Collin went to my father to ask for my hand in marriage.

Although I couldn't exactly explain why I felt the way I did, I still felt it. "I think I would like to be Collin Gentry's wife. He's a man who isn't into things most guys his age are into. He's rock-solid, too. Plus, he's nice to look at."

My father had given me a nod, and I knew that meant he'd tell Collin that he could marry me—if he ever asked.

Parents' weekend had come at the university, and Collin had told me that his parents would be coming to Lubbock to spend the weekend there. But he hadn't asked me if I wanted to meet them yet—which I did, of course.

Saturday morning turned into afternoon, and still no call from Collin. I tried to keep myself occupied by writing an essay for my biology class, but my head wasn't in it. I kept looking out the window, hoping to find Collin driving his truck into the driveway.

A knock came on my bedroom door, making me jump. "Honey, you've got a phone call in your father's office."

Springing to my feet, I ran to the door, throwing it open and running right past my mother. "Thanks, Mom."

My bare feet pounded against the wood floor as I sprinted to my father's office at the far end of the house. There was only one phone, and my father thought it should be in his office in case he had to take calls from his work while at home. He smiled at me as I came in, and I skidded to a stop. Pointing to the phone, which lay on his desk, he said, "I'll give you some privacy, dear."

"Thank you, Daddy." I picked up the phone just as my father closed the door. "Hello?"

"Hello, Fiona. This is Collin Gentry."

I tried not to laugh, as I'd easily recognized his deep voice. "Hello, Collin. How are you doing this afternoon?"

"I'm doing well. My parents arrived a short time ago, and they would like to invite you and your parents to join us for dinner at a restaurant in town. Would you like that?"

"I would love to. Can you hang on a moment while I ask my parents if they're free to go to dinner?"

"I can wait."

Putting the phone down, I raced out of my father's office. "Mom, Dad! Mom, Dad!"

My mother came out of the living room and into the hallway as I ran along it. "For goodness sakes, why are you shouting, dear?"

I stopped running and tried to control my voice. "Mom, do you and Dad have any plans for dinner tonight?"

She folded her arms and cocked her head. "Why do you ask?"

"Because Collin's parents are in town for parents' weekend, and they've invited all of us to go out to dinner with them somewhere here in town."

"Let me ask your father." She walked back into the living room. "Darling, your daughter would like it if we could go to dinner with Collin's parents this evening."

"I heard her talking to you in the hallway." He smiled at me. "And you look as if you'd love us to go."

Clapping my hands, I jumped up and down. "I would adore it if you would go."

"We're free, dear. Tell them we'd love to join them. Get the details, and I'll get us there on time."

Spinning around, I hurried back to the phone, nearly out of breath from all the running. "They said yes, Collin. We would love to meet you for dinner this evening." I sat in Dad's chair, trying to catch my breath as quietly as I could.

"Good. We'll see you at seven at the Fiesta Grill, then.

Bye." And then he hung up, Collin-style. No sweet words of how he'd miss me until he saw me again, nothing but a solid 'bye.'

"Mexican food," I said quietly as I began nibbling my fingernail.

Spicy food and my tummy didn't get along well. And pinto beans gave me gas. But I was sure I could find something on the menu that wouldn't end up making my tummy rumble.

My parents, like most parents, had a steadfast rule—eat everything on your plate. That meant I would have my work cut out for me, finding something to order.

Hours later, with my hair teased so that it stood high and pulled away from my face with a black headband and my bangs pulled forward, I put on a modest amount of makeup. My blue dress made my eyes pop, and pair of black flats finished my ensemble. Mom had put her strand of pearls around my neck to make me look even better.

My parents were dressed nicely as well. We all wanted to make a good first impression on Collin's parents. I'd never been so nervous in my life. "I'm shaking." I held out my hand, and my mother took it into hers.

She held it as we walked into the restaurant. "There's absolutely nothing to be nervous about, Fiona."

She could say that all she wanted, but it didn't make the butterflies inside my stomach swarm any less. "There they are." I spotted Collin, who had just sat down with his parents at a table for six.

Gulping, I looked at the back of his father's head. Dark hair, thick and wavy. I could easily see from where Collin had gotten his. And his mother had a sharply pointed nose—Collin had inherited a male version of it.

As soon as Collin saw us, he stood up and walked to us, shaking my father's hand. "Thank you for coming, Mr. Walton." He nodded at my mother. "Mrs. Walton, thank you for coming."

I waited for him to say something about how nice I looked. "Do you think this dress is okay, Collin?"

He smiled and nodded, then took the hand my mother had just released. "Come, let me introduce you to my parents."

After the introductions were over and done with, Collin pulled out the chair next to his, and I sat down. "Thank you, Collin."

He wasn't always such a gentleman. Often, he'd forget to open the door of his truck for me to get in. He rarely opened doors for me. But he didn't seem to think of doing such things, so I hadn't been completely offended.

He sat down next to me, and the smile he wore told me he was incredibly happy. Collin didn't smile often. And he never smiled for no reason at all. "Fiona is going to become a teacher."

"Is that so?" his mother asked me.

"Yes, ma'am," I said as I smiled at her. "I love children and can't wait to begin my teaching career."

Collin looked at me with a bit of confusion in his dark eyes. "Well, I'm sure you won't always teach. I wouldn't call it a career, Fiona. Someday, you'll have a family to take care of, and you won't be able to work and do that at the same time."

Although what he said bothered me a bit, I was sort of thrilled he was talking about this. "Well, of course my family would always come before anything else. When I have one. If I have one."

My mother laughed. "Certainly, you will have a family someday, Fiona."

My response pleased Collin, and his smile grew even bigger. "Certainly, you will. You would be a great mother."

My cheeks heated with embarrassment as I ducked my head. "Thank you."

His fingers touched my chin, lifting up my face to look at him. "And you'd make a great wife too, Fiona."

My heart stopped. *Is he going to ask me to marry him right here—right now?*

His father spoke, pulling my attention, "In the future. She must finish college and get her degree first."

"Of course," Collin said as he removed his hand from my face.

My flesh burned where he'd touched me. The touch was the most intimate thing he'd ever given me thus far. It felt more intimate than even his chaste kisses on my cheek.

I'd been much closer with the boyfriends I'd had in the past, especially after seeing them for as long as I'd been seeing Collin. I'd talked to them tons in the first few months. But Collin and I didn't talk a whole lot.

When we had a date, we spent the entire time eating, sitting out on the porch swing, listening to the chirping sound of birds, and watching the sun setting in the evening sky. And then he'd bid me goodnight and leave.

All Collin really needed was someone to show him tenderness. I could do that. I could bring out the caring, sensual man in him. If only he'd let me.

As I sat there, talking to his parents and feeling at ease with them in record time, I knew this was something special. This was meant to last. Things like this didn't happen all the time.

It almost felt as if we were already family. Collin's parents were happy we'd found each other, and mine were too. Everyone agreed that Collin and I were a good match for each other. And that made me incredibly happy.

And the way Collin's smile hardly left his face told me that having both of our parents agree on our relationship meant the world to him.

And it meant the world to me too.

❧ 4 ❧

COLLIN

May 1967 – Lubbock, Texas

The end of the school year had come, and I knew it was time to do what I needed to do—even if my heart wasn't entirely in it. Guilt still plagued me whenever I thought about how hurt the girl I'd left behind would feel when she found out about this.

Fiona was everything a wife was supposed to be — in my parents' eyes, at least. My mother did love her, and my father kept telling me how lucky I was that she'd stumbled upon me that fateful evening at the football game. He also kept telling me not to let her get away.

I liked Fiona. I liked her a lot. But love?

Well, love wasn't all it was cracked up to be anyway. My heart still belonged to someone else. But my brain knew that could never be. It kept nagging me to hurry up and make Fiona my wife before someone else swooped in and took her away from me.

I saw other guys looking at her, wondering why she was with me, I was sure. I didn't wine and dine her. I didn't fawn all over her. And I didn't compliment her the way other guys did with their girls. That just wasn't me.

Fiona never complained about that, not even once. She

accepted me for who I was. Don't ask me why, because I do not know. But she did, and that was all I needed.

The last day of classes saw me fingering an engagement ring in my pocket as I made my way to her house. I knew Fiona wasn't home yet, but I wasn't going there to see her anyway.

My heart pounded as I got out of my truck and walked to the front door. *This is it. If her father says yes, then I'll soon be a married man. And that will be that.*

Closing my eyes, I saw the woman I'd left behind. Her dark eyes drooped with sadness as she held her hands out to me. I opened my eyes, knowing that I couldn't take her hands, even if they were real and right in front of me.

She wasn't meant for me.

Fiona would make a good wife; I was sure of it. So, I knocked on the door and waited, shifting my weight from one leg to the other, trying not to seem as nervous as I was.

Mrs. Walton answered the door. "Hello, Collin. I'm afraid that Fiona hasn't made it home yet. But come on in and wait for her."

"Mrs. Walton, I'm not here to see Fiona. I'd like to speak with Mr. Walton if that's okay." It felt like a herd of cattle was stampeding around inside my stomach.

Her blue eyes matched her daughter's, and they went wide as she looked at me with a smile on her lips. "You want to speak with Mr. Walton?"

"Yes, please." My head felt light. I'd never passed out before, but I was sure this was what occurred prior to that.

"Follow me. He's in his office." She led me down the hallway, then tapped on the door to his office. "Honey, Collin's here, and he'd like to speak with you."

"Well, send him in then."

My throat closed up, and I saw black at the edges of my vision as she opened the door and gently pushed me inside. I heard the door close behind me, leaving me and Mr. Walton alone. "Hello, sir."

"Hello, Collin. Have a seat." He gestured to the chair on the other side of the desk he was sitting at.

I shook my head. "I should stand."

With a smile, he winked at me. "Okay then. Why don't you tell me what you came here to talk to me about?"

I pulled the ring out of my pocket and held it up. "I'd like to know if you would give me your permission to ask Fiona to marry me."

He clasped his hands, resting them on his desk. "You'd like to marry my daughter, Collin?"

"Yes, I would like that very much, sir." My mouth was as dry as a cotton ball.

"And if she says yes to your proposal, then would you two be living at the ranch in Carthage?"

I nodded. "Yes, sir."

"Would you two have your own home, or would you be living with your parents?"

"The ranch house is big enough for all of us to live there without getting in each other's way."

"What about Fiona being able to keep her own house? A woman likes to do that. And what about the cooking?"

"We have a cook and maids. Fiona wouldn't have to do any of those things."

"I'm not sure she would like that." He chuckled. "You know, being waited on hand and foot."

"It's not like that. It's just that our house is kept clean, and our laundry is done by the maids. And our meals are cooked by the cook. But we're not ones to ask people to wait on us hand and foot, sir. There are lots to do at the ranch—that's why we have the staff to keep the house and cook for us."

His green eyes narrowed. "Do you love my daughter, Collin?"
Oh, shit!

I had to tell her father that I did love Fiona, or he'd surely say no. So, I opened my mouth, and the lie popped out. "Yes, sir."

The smile he gave me told me he was happy with my answer. "Then I would love to give you my permission to ask Fiona to marry you."

Just then, the door flew open, and there stood Fiona with her mouth gaping. "Collin?"

I tried to shove the ring back into my pocket, but her eyes were already glued on it. "Fiona!"

Moving fast, she came right up to me. "I overheard you talking, Collin." She reached out, wiggling her fingers. "Can I see what you have in your fist?"

I opened my hand, the ring sitting on my palm. "It's for you."

She picked it up off my hand. "It's very pretty."

"I'm glad you like it." I wasn't sure what to say.

Her father cleared his throat. "I'll get out of here and leave you two alone."

With him gone, I felt more comfortable saying what I had to say. "Fiona, your father gave me his blessing, so would you marry me?"

She put the ring on her finger — it was a little big on her. Looking at the ring, she smiled and then looked into my eyes. "I would love to marry you, Collin Gentry."

Relieved that she'd said yes, I let out a long sigh. "Ah, good. We can go see the jeweler and get it fitted properly."

"Good. And while we're there, we can pick out our wedding rings." She reached up, cradling my face between her hands. "Thank you."

Her lips trembled as if she was waiting for a kiss. And I knew it was time to give her a proper one. So, I took her hands, moving them away from my face as I leaned in and pressed my lips to hers.

There was no zing, no electricity. But there wasn't repulsion either, so I thought that a good sign.

A month later, we got married at Whisper Ranch with our

families in attendance. Our mothers cried, and our fathers beamed with pride. Fiona looked beautiful in her white wedding gown. And for the first time, I let her know that. "White suits you, Fiona."

We'd come to my bedroom to spend the first night of our marriage. She turned her back to me. "Can you unzip this for me?"

My hand shook as I gently pulled down the zipper, not wanting to mess up the dress in any way. It was as perfect as she was. "Are you ready for this?"

She nodded. "Yes. Are you?"

I was a man, so I was always ready for sex. "I am."

It had been years since I'd had sex, so I was more than ready for it. But things weren't exactly right yet, even though we were now legally married.

After unzipping her dress, I turned off the light so the dark could hide us from each other. Undressing, I got into bed and soon felt her getting under the blanket with me.

I had thought that when this time would come, I would find it hard not to pounce on my wife. That wasn't happening, though. Instead, I found myself thinking about another woman—one I thought I'd left behind.

Fiona's hand moved slowly across my chest. "It's okay, Collin. I'm ready for this. I've saved my virginity all these years for the man I would marry—for you. What I have is yours now. Take it."

My heart ached as I turned over and put my body on top of hers. Closing my eyes, I went back in time, and suddenly I was with her again—with my Hilda.

With one hard thrust, I broke through the barrier. "Yes," I moaned.

Nails bit into my back as she whimpered, "Oh, God."

Moving, I knew the pain would fade. "You're going to be okay."

"You've done this before?" Fiona asked with surprise, pulling me out of my fantasy.

I wasn't sure what to say. So, I lied. "No. I've just been told that the pain goes away."

"Oh, I see. I like that we're each other's first." She lay with her legs flat against the bed, not moving at all.

I didn't agree since it wasn't true. "Maybe bend your knees. That might help." I knew it would help but didn't want to give my sexual knowledge away.

"I'd rather not."

Doing my best to make some friction between us, I moved faster, not wanting to take too long, as she seemed uncomfortable. "I'll try to hurry."

"Please do."

This wasn't how it was supposed to go. She wasn't supposed to act as if having sex with me was simply another one of her wifely duties—another chore to get through. "I think you're supposed to enjoy this, Fiona."

"At this point, that's impossible. But please enjoy yourself."

Perfect to the point of madness.

"You're too tense, that's why it keeps hurting. You need to relax."

"I can't."

Her body was like a vise, and that made me feel uncomfortable too. "I need you to." I tried to appeal to her need to be a good wife. "Can you try for me?"

With a soft sigh, she whispered, "Collin, it burns like fire between my legs right now. I'm doing my best not to cry. Can you please just do your business so this can be over?"

All I wanted to do was roll off her and get the hell out of that bed. But I didn't do that. I kept moving as she lay stiff as a board under me. I kept going until my body gave in, giving her the ending she wanted so badly. "Ugh!" I grunted as I came.

"Oh, God!" she cried out. But it wasn't with desire or ecstasy.

Pure repulsion filled her voice as she whispered, "That feels so—so…" she seemed unable to find the right word, but then she found it, "…disgusting."

Rolling off her, I got up and went to get a wet washcloth. "I'll get something so you can clean yourself."

"Thank you," came her tear-soaked words. She tried to cry quietly, but I could still hear her.

Disappointment, frustration, and even anger filled me. If she would've just tried to relax and tried to enjoy it, things would've been so different.

I washed my face, which was hot with emotion. Then I wet a washcloth and went back to her, handing it to her. "Here, wash yourself."

"I'm sorry, Collin. I had no idea it would feel so painful and end with such a smelly liquid. I know I'm naïve in the ways of love, but that wasn't at all what I'd expected."

I got into bed feeling completely frustrated with her. "That smelly liquid is called semen, and it makes babies. You do want babies, don't you?"

"Yes." She got out of bed, and when she came back, she had on a nightgown. "Aren't you going to put on something to sleep in?"

"No." I turned over and closed my eyes, trying to push that horrible experience out of my mind.

"I'll wash the bed linens tomorrow. I don't want the maids to have to deal with this disgusting mess."

My teeth ground together as my jaws clenched. She might be naïve to the ways of love, but I wasn't. And this wasn't the way it was supposed to be.

5

COY

July 1988 – Carthage, Texas – Whisper Ranch

Lila and I laid on a pallet on the ground beneath a blanket of stars in one of the back pastures of the ranch. No one came out here, as the cattle had been moved to another pasture to let this one recover for a few months.

We'd seen each other every day since the night we met at my graduation party. And we'd both found that neither one of our families wanted us together. Both her father and mine had forbidden it.

Dad had this archaic notion that our family was better than others in the small town. "When your last name is Gentry, you're expected to live your life a certain way," he'd said, "and you only fraternize with people within your class. And you only date the best young ladies."

My mother wasn't even standing up for me, which I found strange. But she wasn't in good condition at the time, and I thought her weakened state must've been why she didn't have my back.

Lila and I weren't without ideas, though—and we certainly weren't going to let our families get in the way of us being together. We decided to see each other in secret. And when the time would come for me to go away to Lubbock, I'd take her with me.

I wasn't going to be living in the dorms anyway. My father had already bought a house up there for me to live in for the next four years.

Sure, there were still some things to hammer out. Like what I would do with Lila when my parents came to visit. But we'd figure it out. And my father had already promised me a hefty allowance, so I wouldn't have to work and could focus on my classes.

I figured I'd put Lila up in a hotel when my family came to visit. And she was down with that, so things were cool. Eventually, we'd come out with our relationship. But for now, we were keeping it under wraps.

And I was keeping her wrapped in my arms as much as I possibly could. "How come you're so damn easy to love, baby?"

"I could ask you the same thing." She put her hands on my face, then pulled me towards her for a kiss.

Before I knew it, I was on top of her, trying to rid her of her clothes so I could get to that soft and creamy flesh of hers. Nothing had ever felt as right as being with Lila did. I knew she was it for me. I knew it—without a doubt.

What I didn't understand was why our families were so against us. Sure, my father had given me his reasons—that our family was better than Lila's—that we were above them. But that was bullshit.

I was more curious about why Lila's family was also so against us being together. I thought they might be upset that my family were assholes. But that wasn't reason enough to hate me.

And they did hate me.

Lila had taken me to meet her family the day after the party. She'd had no idea they would react negatively. And I hadn't told her a thing about what my father had said to me that first night either.

Everyone was all smiles until I told them my last name. Her father had immediately asked the name of my father, and I told him, never thinking that he would have an issue with him. But he did.

I had no idea what it was because he wouldn't tell me or Lila. He just told me that I wasn't welcome in his home and that I was forbidden to speak to his daughter.

Lila and I knew one thing—our families were both hiding something. And it seemed to be a deep, dark secret. There was no other reason for them to forbid a relationship between us.

But that was something to worry about later. Despite the problems we faced with our families, everything felt easy—and right—when we were together. We tried our best not to let those worries intrude.

Lila unbuttoned my shirt, moving her hands over my chest as she pushed me off her, only to climb on top of me and sitting up. Her breasts looked gorgeous in the moonlight—full, supple, and juicy.

She smiled down at me as her long, dark hair cascaded around her shoulders. "Coy, what will you do if our families find out about us?"

"I'll do whatever I have to do to keep you." I wasn't about to let them get in our way. "I know it's only been a little over a month since we met, but I love you."

"Me too." She sighed and looked up at the sky. "Can't you give us a break, God?"

I took her by the wrists, pulling her down to me until our lips met. I knew God had already given us so much, allowing us to meet. I wasn't going to ask him for more than what he'd already given.

I rolled back over, pinning her to the ground beneath me. "Lila, my father can take away everything, and I still wouldn't let you go. I never want you to worry about my commitment to you."

"My father hasn't ever given me anything he can take away.

About all he can do is disown me and tell me to leave his home. But that's not really such a threat." She laughed. "I know it's different for you, though. You stand to inherit all of Whisper Ranch. And you'd be giving up so much more."

"I. Love. You," I reiterated, emphasizing each word with a kiss. "You are all I want in this world. Money isn't worth losing you over."

She stared into my eyes, looking into them in a way I was sure was meant to find the truth. "You would give it all up for me?"

"I would." I hoped it wouldn't come to that, but I wouldn't be bullied by money. "You know, the only thing that really bothers me is that I'd lose my parents. Mom, especially. Dad's always been a hard ass. But I've always thought that he did what he thought was best for me. Now, I'm not so sure."

"He sent you away to go to school. I think that was harsh."

"Yeah. I was only six."

"I can't imagine being away from my mother and father when I was that age. You must've been afraid when they left you there —that school looks so big and impersonal."

I'd taken her to see the place where I'd lived for so long. She'd compared it to growing up in an orphanage. It wasn't quite that bad, but it wasn't like growing up at home, with my family.

"I was afraid. I cried every night for the first month. And then, when I realized that my father wasn't going to let me come back home for anything more than brief visits, I stopped crying. I accepted it." And I knew that I could live my life without my parents being a part of it—if it came to that. My father had made sure I knew how to live without them.

"I'll never leave you, Coy." The way her hands moved over my back comforted me. No one had ever comforted me the way Lila could. Not even my mother.

I'd always felt closer to Mom. Growing up, I'd watched as she was forced to accept my father's will over and over again. She was as much a victim as I was. But she was strong in many ways, and he didn't run over her nearly as much as he did over me. I'd been a kid then, though. Now, at eighteen, I was considered a man. My father couldn't rule over me any longer.

Pushing her silky hair away from her face, I looked at her. She was worth losing everything—even my parents. "I will never leave you, Lila. And one day, we will make this official. I can't wait to marry you, you know."

Lila had two more weeks before she turned eighteen. "I can't wait to marry you, Coy. I would be more than happy to go down to the courthouse and file our marriage license the day I turn eighteen."

I wondered what our families would do if we just ran off, gotten married, and then went back home. They couldn't do much, I thought. It would be a done deal, and they would just have to get over themselves.

"I don't want to hide you away any longer. And I don't want to hide you away in Lubbock either. I think we should get married before the summer is over. That way, I can take you to Lubbock with me as my wife. It makes me feel bad that we have to hide things, even now. I don't want to keep doing it."

"People will call us crazy," she told me.

"Well, I *am* crazy. Over you." I smiled, then kissed her. Her kisses transported me to a place beyond earthly understanding. And I knew I wanted to go everywhere with her from now on.

To hell with our families. All that really matters is the two of us.

✣ 6 ✣

FIONA

December 1967 – Carthage, Texas – Whisper Ranch

Six months into our marriage, Collin began disappearing at night. Not every night, though. About every third or fourth night, I'd wake, and he'd be gone. Not wanting to wander around the huge house and risk waking people up, I'd stay in bed, awake, wondering where he'd gone.

He stayed away so long that I would eventually fall asleep, only to wake with him sleeping soundly in our bed. He'd always be naked and would reek of sexual activity.

My hopes were that he was somewhere pleasing himself and not having relations with someone else. Thus far, I hadn't been able to bring myself to talk to him about what he was doing.

I didn't find sex comfortable in the least. I could feel his frustration with me each time we had sex, which was once a week on Sunday nights.

I'd go to church each Sunday morning with his mother— Collin and his father never joined us. I found that odd since he'd come to church with me and my parents the entire year we were in Lubbock. But once we'd gotten back to his home, things changed.

I was the one who had made Sunday nights the night we'd

have sex. And it was purely to make a baby and nothing else. I had no idea why I found sex to be so disgusting, but I did.

I hated the heat of his semen when it flushed into my body. And I found the smell so foul that it always made my stomach hurl, and I had to try my best not to gag.

So when he came back to bed, stinking of the stuff, I would always sleep with my head under the pillow to block the stench.

After a month of him leaving our bed, I finally felt I should ask him what was going on. I woke up to find him gone again, but this time I stayed up until he came back into the bedroom.

When he opened the door and found me sitting up in bed with the lamp on, he looked like a deer in the headlights. "What are you doing awake, Fiona?"

"I think it's time you tell me what has you getting out of bed in the dead of night only to return hours later smelling of semen." I crossed my arms over my chest and waited for his answer.

In an instant, his face turned red. "None of your damn business." He strode to the bathroom, turning on the shower. I found that odd, as he'd never done that before.

I sat in bed, tears stinging the backs of my eyes as thoughts filled my mind. There were some young maids who worked and lived in the house. *Is he sneaking out to have sex with one of them?*

Getting out of bed, I went to the bathroom. Opening the door, I found the glass shower door covered in steam so thick that I could barely make out his silhouette. "Collin, I know that I don't please you when we have sex. Are you sleeping with one of the maids?"

"No," he barked. "And you don't even *try* to please me."

"I'm sorry. I don't know how to make myself feel differently."

"You just lay there, stiff as a board. It's not easy for me to even have an orgasm. And then you make that horrible sound every time I ejaculate."

I hadn't realized that he'd heard my gagging. I'd tried hard

32

not to do it, but it must've been escaping my mouth without my knowledge. "I'm sorry. I really am. And I'll try harder not to do that."

He'd said he hadn't been sleeping with one of the maids, and that made me feel better. But not by much.

"Why can't you at least bend your knees?" He turned the water off, and I turned my back to him so I wouldn't see him naked.

I hadn't liked the few glimpses I'd gotten of his manhood hanging between his legs. "It feels awkward when you make me try that."

"Why are you turning away from me?"

"Because you're naked, and I don't want to make you feel self-conscious." I thought it was a nice thing for me to do.

But he obviously didn't. "Turn around and look at your husband, Fiona Gentry."

Taking a deep breath, I did as he asked, making sure to keep my eyes above his waistline. "There, are you happy now?"

He moved his hand to hold his penis. "Look at this."

I didn't want to look at it. "Collin, stop."

"No," he shouted. "Look at this." He moved his hand, shaking his manhood as if trying to taunt me with it.

"You're being disgusting." I walked back to the bed and got under the blanket. "Have you been drinking?" I thought he must have been downstairs, getting drunk, and probably playing with himself—which made me sick.

"A bit." He came towards the bed, naked.

I turned the lamp off so I didn't have to witness his penis swinging around between his legs. "Let's just go to sleep. I'm tired."

"You shouldn't have stayed up waiting for me to come back to bed. *Our* bed." He flopped down onto the bed, making the springs moan under his weight. And then he moved some more, making them squeak and squeak.

"What are you doing?"

"This is what it's supposed to sound like when two people have sex on a bed."

"Please go to sleep. You're inebriated."

"You know, if it makes you so sick to have sex with me, maybe you should just get on your hands and knees so you don't have to face me when we do it."

Picturing what he'd suggested, I felt as if I might throw up. "You want to mount me like an animal?"

"That's one way of putting it. We should try that right now. Get on your knees."

I wasn't about to have sex with him. "It's Tuesday, not Sunday. Perhaps I'll want to try that horrible position then. I doubt it, though. Missionary is the best way. Sex is to make babies, and nothing else."

"You're wrong. And you're even wrong about that position. In the pictures, the woman bends her knees," he let me know.

"In the pictures?" I got the idea that he was looking at some pornographic magazines while playing with himself.

"Yes. There are pictures of people having sex. And in all the pictures I've seen, the woman is bending her knees. And guess what—there are many more positions. That's not the only one."

I didn't want to talk about this any longer. "Can we just go to sleep now?"

He turned to face me, leaning his head on his hand as he raised his upper body to look down at me. "Why does talking about sex with your husband disturb you so much?"

"It's not appropriate." I felt my cheeks heat with embarrassment.

"If it's not appropriate to talk with *me* about sex, then *who* is it appropriate for you to talk about this with? Because you need to talk to someone about your problem." His chest rose and fell as he sighed.

One tear escaped me, slowly sliding down my cheek. He

made me feel like I was on trial. "It's *not* a problem, Collin. We have sex. If you want me to bend my knees, then I will."

"Good, let's try that now." He threw the blanket off me, then pulled at the hem of my gown to rid me of it.

But I wasn't having any of that. Instead, I held the gown tightly in my hands. "Not tonight."

"Why not?" He smiled at me. "Sunday isn't the only night we can do this."

"We're not doing this tonight because you are clearly drunk." I could smell the slight scent of whiskey on his hot breath. And I felt sure he'd already given himself an orgasm. "Plus, you've already spent yourself."

"I've got plenty left for you." He ran his hand over my shoulder as if trying to seduce me.

"Collin, please stop. I want to sleep."

"Come on," he said with a chuckle as if he thought himself funny. "Let's just get crazy and wild."

"I feel as if you aren't listening to me. I'm not going to have sex with you tonight. End of discussion. Go to sleep." Rolling onto my side, I turned my back to him.

"Fine." The bed creaked as he moved to lie on his side, turning his back to me as well.

This isn't the way I pictured our marriage at all.

❧ 7 ❧

COLLIN

I had no idea Fiona would turn out to be such a damn prude. If I had, I wouldn't have married her. I was a man, after all. A man with the same needs as any other man.

It was now obvious to me that Fiona wasn't ever going to like sex.

I'd tried for months—for years—to forget about Hilda. But when Fiona proved to be more than a disappointment in the bedroom, I found myself driving to Hilda's small apartment on the other side of town—the wrong side of town.

She didn't ask me a thing when I first went to her. She just opened the door and let me take her into my arms as if no time had passed at all.

Hilda didn't care that I would come to her late at night. We'd have amazing, insane sex, and then I'd leave. And Hilda never complained, not even once.

She saw the wedding ring on my finger, and I saw the pained look in her dark eyes. But she didn't ask me anything.

I hadn't meant for things to keep going between us. I knew it was selfish of me, but I thought I'd only need Hilda until my wife found her sexual footing. Once that happened, I thought I would stop going to her. I'd be able to get everything a man needed at home.

I liked to get rough with Hilda, but I knew better than to think I could ever do that with a good woman like my wife. All I'd wanted from her was some okay sex. But it seemed as if that was a pipe dream.

It also seemed that seeing Hilda wasn't going to end. I wasn't sure how to feel about that either. It had been much different, sneaking around to see Hilda when I was young and single. Now that I was older and married, it lacked the thrill it did before. Now it seemed downright dangerous.

If I was caught having an affair with another woman, it wouldn't be good. If I was caught having an affair with Hilda, a woman my family considered beneath me, it meant that I should expect the worst.

My father might well disown me if this ever came out. I might end up on the streets with nothing, and Fiona would end up getting all my inheritance. I knew my father well enough to know that he would add insult to injury if I defied his wishes. He'd throw me to the wolves before he'd listen to why I'd gone to her in the first place.

Fiona lived up to the role expected of my wife in every way, except where sex was concerned. She was devoted to me in every way, save one. She had no interest in pleasing me in bed nor in allowing me to please her.

Is there something wrong with Fiona?

I laid there with my back to her, trying to figure out what I'd done wrong, and began to switch gears. Maybe Fiona needed to see a doctor. Perhaps if a doctor told her it was okay to enjoy having sex with her husband, then she'd look at it in a different light.

I knew one thing for certain. I wanted an heir. I wanted children. And I knew I had to make things better between us.

Flipping over, I ran my hand over her shoulder, trying to be comforting. "Fiona, I think you need to see a doctor."

"What?" She turned to lie on her back, looking at me with wide eyes.

"You need to see a doctor. Sex should feel good for you. I don't think things are working right for you. Were you ever injured in that area?" There had to be some scientific explanation for her frigidity.

"No!" She shook her head indignantly. "I really don't want to have this conversation." She closed her eyes, her cheeks turning scarlet.

"I know you don't. But you're going to have this conversation with a doctor. You'll need to get examined thoroughly by a doctor to make sure nothing is wrong." I didn't know what else to do—I figured it was time for professional help.

"You mean that I *have* to go see a doctor and let him look at my privates?" Another shake of her head sent her blonde hair flying around her face. "No! Never!"

"Fiona, what do you think is going to happen to you when you get pregnant?" I had to wonder how she thought things like that worked. It was now clear to me that she was very naïve about all of this.

"I don't know. I don't care either. All I know is that I will deal with that when the time comes. For now, I *don't* have to deal with that. Nothing is wrong with me."

I went to put on some pajamas, as I no longer wished to be naked anywhere near my wife. "I'm not going to beg you to let me please you."

"Good." She turned back on her side and pulled up the blanket to cover all but her head. "I'm going to sleep."

After putting on my pajamas, I got into bed and tried not to think of the events of the night. I'd had such a good time before I came back home. Hilda had gone down on me, and I'd exploded in her mouth. And she'd loved it as much as I had.

Hilda let me do anything I wanted to her, and she loved everything I did to her, including whipping her sweet ass until it turned a rosy red.

If I ever even said a thing to Fiona about spanking her sweet ass, she'd chew me up and spit me out. She and I were not compatible as lovers, that was for sure.

Fiona sighed as I got back into bed, then turned to face me. "I know you expect me to be more daring in the bedroom. So, I will try. I'll bend my knees. I'll even let you take me from behind. But I don't want to do anything else. It…doesn't feel right to me."

"You're missing out." I thought she should know that. "You really should see a doctor."

"I will see a doctor when I'm pregnant, but not before that. You can have me more than one way now, so be satisfied with that."

"I want to have sex with you three times a week, or even more. If you say that sex is only to make babies, then I want to make sure we make some. As your husband, I expect you to participate in this."

She made a loud sigh. "Fine. You can have sex with me every night if you feel it will help us conceive. But only in the ways I've stated."

"Foreplay will help stimulate you—help you enjoy it more." She didn't seem to know the basics about sex and conception. "I've been raising cattle and horses for quite a while now. When one cow comes into season, it forces the others to join in as well. The bull changes how he acts with them too. He's more playful with the cows, and there's plenty more physical contact before he actually mounts them."

"I've been at the ranch long enough to have witnessed that. And what I've seen is that the cows try to get away from the bull. It seems to me that his attention is more of a bother to them than anything." She wasn't going to budge.

"Fine, Fiona. But don't be surprised when I let myself go and let out a moan or two when we're doing it doggy-style."

"Please, don't call it that. This is already hard enough for me."

Why does she have to be such a fucking prude?

❧ 8 ❧

FIONA

1969 – Carthage, Texas – Whisper Ranch

Two years went by with no pregnancy. I'd gotten used to the sex. It never got to the point where I liked it, but I'd gotten used to it. Collin had gone from wanting sex every night for the first month of us trying to have a baby to being fine with twice a week. Sunday nights and Wednesday nights, we'd have sex twice, once when going to bed and once in the middle of the night when he'd wake me up by climbing on top of me.

It seemed as if he had a mission, and finally, the mission was accomplished. I came into the living room, where Collin and his parents were sitting after dinner. I'd gone to the doctor a week before and had gone back that day to find out what the test results were. I had the paper in my hand and hoped the news would be joyful for everyone.

Collin didn't even look up at me as I walked into the room. His mother did, though, shifting her attention away from the knitting in her lap. "Hello, dear." Her eyes went to the paper in my hand. "What do you have there?"

"I have something that will change our lives around here a little." I knew a baby would make quite a difference in the house; there hadn't been a little one in it since Collin was a baby.

Mother Gentry looked at her son. "Listen up, Collin. It seems that your wife has something to show us."

He raised his eyes from the book he'd been reading. "And what's that?"

I held the paper out as I went towards him, handing it to him. "Here you go. Read it yourself."

He looked the page over as his dark brows rose. "You've gone to see a doctor."

"I have." I couldn't wipe the smile off my face.

He smiled too. "And this says that you had a pregnancy test done last week."

"I did." I swayed back and forth as I waited for him to say the words I'd been waiting to hear.

"And this says that the test results were positive." He put the paper down as he looked at me. "We're having a baby?"

Nodding, I said, "We are."

Suddenly his mother was behind me, hugging me, and his father stood up, his eyes shining. Collin was the only one who didn't get up. Instead, he put the paper down and nodded. "Good. You've finally done what a wife is supposed to do."

His mother let me go as we both stared at Collin with gaping mouths. She finally asked, "Aren't you going to get up and give your wife a hug?"

"Why?" He picked the book back up. "For doing what God made her to do?"

His dispassionate reaction wasn't something I'd been prepared for; I ran out of the room as my eyes clouded with tears. I went right up the stairs, straight to our bedroom.

I slammed the door behind me, then ran to the bed and crashed onto it, sobbing into my pillow. "How can he be so mean?"

I'd given my husband the best news a wife could possibly give her husband, and he had acted as if it meant nothing to him. I didn't understand the man at all.

I hadn't heard him come into our bedroom with all my crying, but a hand on my shoulder let me know he had. "Fiona, why in the world are you crying?"

Sitting up, I had to restrain myself from slapping him—I wanted to so badly. "How can you ask me such a thing? I told you that we're going to have a baby, and you don't seem to care at all. It's been two years since we began trying so hard to make this baby. Two years, Collin! And you can't muster enough emotion to even give me a hug and tell me that you're happy."

"Of course I'm happy. You know I want kids. I don't understand why you would think otherwise." He sat on the bed beside me, running his hand through my hair. "I just meant that your body finally decided to do what it was made to do, bear children."

"And why is it that you think this long wait was due to *my* body and not *your* sperm?" I knew he was still pleasuring himself at least once or twice a week. Countless nights I'd woken to find him gone, coming back before sunrise. "You haven't been storing it up, after all."

He cocked his head. "What do you mean by that?"

"I mean that you've been playing with yourself—no doubt looking at porno magazines and ejaculating. That could well be the reason why it took us so long to conceive, rather than it being any fault of mine. The doctor performed an exam on me, and he found nothing wrong."

His brows shot up. "He did?" His jaws tightened. "And how did this exam go, exactly?"

I was immensely proud of myself for how trusting I'd been with the doctor. "Last week, when I went for the pregnancy test, he asked me if I'd ever had a pelvic exam, and I told him that I hadn't. He replied that I would need one to make sure my reproductive system was in good working order."

"And he found that it is?" he asked.

"He did." But I'd told my doctor more. "Once he told me that

43

everything looked great, I told him about my lack of enthusiasm where sex is concerned, and he asked me to lie back and close my eyes while he did some tests."

With narrowed eyes, he asked, "What kinds of tests did he do?"

"Professional ones." I didn't like the way he looked at me. "Anyway, he used this instrument to stimulate a sexual organ he called a clitoris, and it worked."

"He gave you an orgasm?" shock filled his voice, and anger filled his eyes.

"Yes." I didn't understand why he was so angry. "Look, he said that the reason I probably don't like having sex with you has something to do with your attitude toward me. So, you might want to see what you can do about that." He had to realize that, as a woman, I needed more than he was giving—and not just physically. "You don't compliment me." The doctor had asked me a lot of questions about our relationship and how we communicated. He had been very kind and attentive, and he said that my aversion to having sex with Collin could have lots to do with how we treated each other outside of the bedroom.

"Never have," he agreed. "That never bothered you when we dated."

"Well, we weren't having sex then. I suppose a girl needs to hear nice things from her husband now and then if she's to enjoy having sex with him." And there'd been more the doctor had told me. "I also told him about how you're pleasuring yourself at least twice a week, and he said that's like a slap in the face to a woman. So there's another reason why I might not enjoy having sex with you."

"I didn't do that at the beginning of our marriage, and you know it." He got off the bed and went to stand at its end, seemingly to get away from me.

"Look, you're taking this all wrong. I'm just telling you these things so we can change them. So we can try to change our love-

44

life. That's what the doctor said. He said that we have to be honest with each other if we want a happy marriage and a healthy sex-life. Don't you want that with me?"

"Take your clothes off." He folded his arms over his chest.

I wasn't sure what he was getting at. "Why?"

"Because you let that man play with you, but you won't let me do that. You told me that you don't like being touched down there. But you clearly do. Just not by your husband—the *one* man who is *supposed* to touch you there."

"You're jealous?" I asked with confusion. "Of a doctor?"

"A doctor who gave my wife her first and only orgasm. And furthermore, you did this a week ago, so you've been hiding it from me this whole time. How many times have we had sex since this doctor diddled you?"

"Don't say it like that. He didn't use his fingers. He used a machine. A medical device." I hated how ugly he was making this.

"That machine is called a vibrator, Fiona. And it's not just a medical device. Answer my question."

"Twice. You and I have had sex twice since my appointment." I didn't see why that mattered.

"So, you had two chances to tell me what went on between you and this doctor—who, by the way, you are never to see again."

I didn't like his tone—or what he was saying—but I was still stuck on something he'd said earlier. "How do you know that the medical device is called a vibrator?"

"Everyone knows that, Fiona. Lots of people use them. Not just doctors. To be honest with you, I had no idea that they used them to give their patients orgasms. What's next, more appointments to get orgasms?"

"I don't think so. I didn't get one today if that's what you're thinking." But the doctor had told me that I might think about getting myself an auto-stimulator. Not that I was about to tell my incredibly angry husband about that.

"How come you still have your clothes on?" He looked at me up and down. "I want you naked right now."

We both knew he couldn't give me an orgasm. "And what do you want to do to me?"

"You don't trust me."

"I know."

Pain filled his dark eyes. "Why don't you trust me? Have I ever hurt you?"

"I don't think you do it on purpose, but yes. You've hurt me almost every time we've had sex. You're too rough." I had never meant to tell him that, but he had asked.

His jaw clenched, and his hands fisted at his sides. "I'm not rough with you. You have no idea what rough sex is. I would show you, but you obviously are much too fragile for that."

"Reading all that nasty pornography has warped your mind, Collin. You should stop doing that. I've seen some of them, you know. And no one in real life does all the things those nasty people in those horrible magazines do."

"How do I hurt you?"

"You push too hard. You just shove your penis into me, and it hurts right from the beginning, and it keeps hurting until the end."

"I tried to get your juices flowing before inserting myself into you, but you said you hated it. And yet, you allowed some other man to do so. You let him have your only orgasm." He thumbed his chest. "That belonged to me, and you gave it away like it was nothing. That thing between your legs is mine and only mine. Do you understand me? You will never allow anyone—not even a fucking doctor—to stimulate anything on your body ever again. That is *mine*, and only *I* will be stimulating you. Now take your fucking clothes off so I can show you what I can do for you."

"No." I wasn't about to let him touch me. "I don't like your attitude about this, Collin. And I'm not about to give myself to you when you're so angry. Maybe when you calm down—but not right now."

"Because I've hurt you before."

"Yes."

Turning away from me, he walked to the door. "I'm going to go have some drinks."

"Great." I was far from happy about that. It meant he'd come home drunk and try to have sex with me. He was always rougher with me after he'd been drinking. But I was happy for him to be gone for a while. "I'll be right here."

"Where a wife belongs." And with that, he closed the door, leaving me alone.

COLLIN

The day I learned I was going to be a father should've been the happiest day of my life. Only it wasn't, because my frigid wife had let her doctor give her her first orgasm.

I poured another shot of whisky down my throat before getting off the barstool. "That's it. I'm going to show her."

As I drove out of the parking lot, I took a left instead of the right that would take me back to the ranch and back to my wife. I didn't want to see her yet. I was still too angry.

So I drove to Hilda's. I'd bought her a small house, still on the wrong side of town. If I'd put her up in a house on the right side of town, people would've started asking questions.

Not only was the house on the wrong side of town, but it was out of the city limits too. The driveway had huge salt cedar trees that flanked it, hiding the house and the parking area from prying eyes. That way, no one would accidentally find me at her place.

As soon as I drove up, the front door opened, and there she stood, waiting for me as always. Hilda never complained—even though she had every right to.

I got out of my truck and went to her. She stepped back to let me inside. "You seem upset, Collin."

"That's because I am." I'd never talked to Hilda about

my wife or marriage. It didn't seem like a thing to talk to a mistress about. But I had to talk to someone. "She said I hurt her when we have sex. She let a fucking doctor give her an orgasm last week. I haven't even gotten one out of the frigid bitch, and she let some other man take what is mine!"

"I see." She went to pour me a drink.

"I know how to give a woman an orgasm."

"Yes, you do." She handed me the glass.

I took a sip. The hot whisky burned as it went down my throat. "She's too fragile, that's what she is. She'd rather someone use a vibrator on her than their mouth."

"She's a fool." She took a seat on the sofa, curling her legs underneath her.

Hilda was thick and curvy, her caramel skin supple and shining under the minimal light that came from the kitchen behind her.

Hilda was like home to me. She was easy to be with. She was easy to fuck. And she never complained.

"What she really needs is a firm hand." I put the glass down as I went to Hilda. "Like the one I give you."

"You're right." She ducked her head. "If you need to take out your anger for her on me, then I am yours to do with as you please, Master."

My body heated with her selfless words. Hilda accepted her role as my submissive with so much ease and pleasure. Fiona would never accept this part of me. I would never even let my wife see this side of me. I was dark as night — something Fiona had no inkling of.

But there was a part of me that wondered if the dominant in me could actually bend my wife's will to make it suit me. "If only I could whip her just once, then she'd watch the words that roll off her tongue far too easily."

"You're right."

I ran my hand over her bowed head. "If I could go down on her only once, she'd bend to my will."

"You're right."

"I own you."

"You do."

"And I own her as well."

"You do."

"So why can't I do to her the things I do to you?"

"Because she's not your submissive, Master. She is your wife."

She was right about that. Fiona was an educated woman who had opinions on everything. She knew what she wanted and how she wanted them. And she wanted as little to do with my dick as possible.

"I shouldn't have let her get that teaching job at the elementary school." I'd never allowed Hilda to work since I came back to Carthage. Why I'd let my wife work was beyond me. "She was already too headstrong, and the job has made her even more so."

As I stood in front of Hilda, she knew just what to do. She began undoing my jeans, pushing them down so that they pooled around my ankles. She took my cock in her very capable hands before looking up at me. "May I suck your cock, Master?"

Looking down at her soulful eyes, I nodded. "You may."

A soft smile curled her lips, and she licked them before setting to work. As always, she took me away from my thoughts, and everything became good again.

I smoothed my hand over her silky dark hair, loving the way it felt beneath my palm. Everything about Hilda did something for me; from her unending devotion to the way she took care of my every sexual need.

Society had rules that I didn't seem to be able to live by for long periods. I had always found my way back to Hilda and the decadent life we had.

After she'd done her job and drank down my juices, she stood up as I sat down, trying to catch my breath. She left me only for a moment and then returned with a leather belt in her hand and nothing on her body.

Handing me the belt, she lay over my lap, presenting her bare ass to me. "Whip her, Master. Whip your wife for her betrayal."

I bent the supple leather in half, then pulled it up high, letting it fall against her caramel-colored flesh. "Count your lashes."

"One," she whispered.

"Do you know why I am punishing you?" I raised the belt again.

"Because I allowed another man to take what was yours and yours alone."

I whipped her again. "Yes."

"Two."

Raising the belt once more, I asked, "Did you enjoy what that man did to you?"

"I did."

I whipped her again as anger ripped through me. "Ten more lashes then."

"Three."

I gave her three more in rapid succession. "Am I not enough for you?"

"You are," she said. "Four, five, six."

I hit her three more times. "How could you do that to me?"

"Seven, eight, nine," she said quietly. "I was thoughtless."

"Five more lashes then." I quickly gave them to her.

"Ten, eleven, twelve, thirteen, four—" her voice broke as a sob escaped her lips, "—teen."

"You sound as if you understand me now. You've got two more coming to you." I hit her once.

"Fif—" she sobbed, "—teen." Her body shook as she cried hopelessly.

I gave her the last one. "There. Your punishment has been served by your master. What do you say to your master?"

"Sixteen," she said with tears flowing, her voice cracked. "Thank you, Master."

Had it been Fiona on my lap, I might not have given her so many lashes. But I knew Hilda could take the harsh punishment since I'd trained her for years. I knew she enjoyed receiving it as much as I loved giving it.

I put the belt down beside me, then ran my hands over her red bottom. "If you didn't betray my trust, I wouldn't have had to do that."

"Yes, I understand. I was bad."

Pulling her cheeks apart, I leaned over, running my tongue along the crack of her ass. "For the next part of your punishment, I will fuck your asshole orally, and you may not orgasm as I do it. If you do, it will mean twenty more lashings for you. One at a time, painstakingly slow. Do you understand me?"

"I do, Master."

I moved one hand under her to manipulate her clit while I tongue-fucked her asshole. And like the trained submissive that she was, she took it all and never came.

Hilda was something to be proud of, yet I couldn't tell a soul about her. She took all I had to give, and she made me a better man by doing it.

But I wasn't a better man to my wife, who lay crying on our bed at home. I wasn't a better man to my wife, who now carried my child. I wasn't a better man to her because this woman on my lap—this woman who was so ready to take the punishment that my wife should've gotten—ruled my heart and my cock.

Anger flooded me, and I picked Hilda up, then lay her out on the sofa. Looking down at her, I saw torture on her face. "You want to come, don't you?"

She nodded. "But I won't."

"You were right to take the punishment meant for her, you know that, don't you?"

She nodded. "I do."

"If you were not the temptress that you are, then I wouldn't be here, cheating on my pregnant wife. If you weren't the evil slut that you are, I wouldn't be here with you so many nights when I should be in bed with my wife. You're a filthy whore, that's what you are. And you've stolen my heart. I don't have it to give to the woman I'm married to. You've ruined our sex-life."

"I am sorry."

"You will be, you dirty whore."

Standing, I took the rest of my clothes off, then picked her up by the hair, and flung her to the floor. She landed on her back, and I pounced on her, shoving my fat cock into her tender pussy. A pussy so swollen with arousal that it made it hard for me to get all the way in. But I pushed and thrust until I was balls deep in the bitch.

She clawed my back as I fucked her with no mercy. "Please," she begged.

"Please what?" I bit her on the neck.

Her nails clawed me once more. "Please, don't."

"Don't what, you nasty bitch?" I bit her earlobe as I slammed into her again and again.

"Don't stop loving me, Master." She sobbed. "I can't live without you."

Slowing down, I looked at her, watching the tears running down the sides of her face. "As if I could, you seductress. As if you would allow that for even a second. My heart is yours, and you damn well know it."

"And mine is yours, and it always will be." She caressed my cheeks, pulling me in to kiss her.

Our tongues tangled as she arched her body to mine. I didn't know where I ended and she began—we were so much a part of one another.

As I took her for what was surely the millionth time, I wondered if my wife and I would ever share what my submissive and I did. A love so pure that it had an abundance of patience and the never-ending desire to glue us together as one entity.

Our bodies gave in to each other, and I collapsed on top of her, trying to catch my breath as she tried to catch hers. I would never share this type of intimacy with my wife. And for that, I was sad.

Fiona carried my child, and yet I felt more a part of Hilda than I had ever felt with Fiona.

And I couldn't imagine that changing.

10

LILA

July 1988 – Carthage, Texas

One day after my eighteenth birthday, I met Coy at the courthouse, where we bought our marriage license. The clerk behind the desk smiled as she said, "You have to wait three days before you can legally get married. This license is only good for ninety days, so you have to get married before time runs out."

"We're going to come back up here and let the Justice of the Peace marry us in three days," Coy informed her.

"Okay then. He'll know that the signed license has to be turned in within thirty days of the legal marriage." She beamed at us. "You two make a cute couple. I'm sure you'll be happy together. Congratulations!"

Coy handed me the paper. "You hold onto this. Keep it in your purse so we'll have it when we come back."

Even though I was the happiest I'd ever been, there was still a ton of nerves bubbling in my tummy as we walked to the doors of the courthouse. "Okay, I'll have it with me when we come back." I hated that we couldn't be seen together; we were taking a huge risk just by being in the courthouse together. "I'll leave first, and then you take off in fifteen minutes."

He nodded, pulled me to him, and kissed me. "Soon, all this sneaking around will be a thing of the past."

"I hope so. I really do." Carefully placing the marriage license into a zippered pouch inside my purse so no one would accidentally see it, I zipped up my purse, then walked out the door.

Looking around, I made sure that no one I knew was around before taking off. My house was half a mile away, and I had to walk all the way.

I couldn't have asked my father if I could borrow the car—he would've wanted to know why. So, I'd taken off on foot, telling my mother that I was walking over to one of my friend's houses to hang out with them.

As I walked along the sidewalk a few minutes later, I heard the familiar sound of Coy's truck as he drove past me. He gunned the engine playfully, making me smile.

Coy was the best-looking guy I'd ever dated—or even knew, for that matter. He had bigger muscles than any guy I'd gone to school with too. He said that was because of the rigorous exercise regimen they did at his boarding school, which focused a lot on sports.

But the thing that really set Coy Gentry apart from all the other boys I'd ever known was his sweetness. He was kind, gentle, and caring. He was also much more mature than any guy I'd met. I chalked it up to having to live away from home since he was a little kid. He'd had to grow up fast and learned not to depend on others for ordinary things like comfort and even love.

Coy had loads of love to give, and I thanked my lucky stars that I got to be one of its recipients. Life with him as my husband was going to be amazing. There wasn't a doubt in my mind.

I knew things had moved fast for us. And I knew that that alone would've been cause for concern for my family. But I also put the blame for our rushed marriage squarely on their shoulders.

If our families could've stayed out of our business and not let whatever feud they had to interfere with our relationship, then we would've had more time to date before rushing into marriage.

This was their fault, not ours.

My hope was that everyone would accept us once we were married, and there was nothing they could do about it. But that was a long-shot, and both of us were aware of it.

Coy had been preparing for the worst. He'd pulled money out of the bank account his father had opened for him when he had turned sixteen. Being afraid that someone might find it if he stashed the cash in his house, he'd given it to me to hide. Again, my purse was serving as our hiding place.

He'd withdrawn the money in hundred-dollar bills, so the stack wasn't that thick. Still, there was so much of it in my wallet that it was getting hard to close.

I knew I would have to get an envelope to store whatever else he ended up taking out of the bank account. I hadn't even dared to count the cash we had so far.

When I got to the next crosswalk, I saw Coy parked in a used parking lot down the street and wondered what he was up to. Heading that way, I wanted to check things out. Not that I could walk up to him in public in the light of day.

Walking by slowly, I acted as if I wasn't looking his way, but I still caught some action out of the corner of my eye. But what I saw had me stopping and turning my head all the way to look at Coy, who was taking a set of car keys from the salesman.

Coy walked over to a tan Honda Accord, got inside, and started it up. I walked around the corner to hide myself from view as I watched him drive it around the block and back into the parking lot.

My heart raced as I saw him get out, nodding as he and the salesman spoke. Then, they went into the office, and I had a distinct impression that Coy was going to buy the car. And I also had the impression that he was going to give it to me.

My mother didn't even own her own car. No one I knew had

their own car. There were family cars—everyone had one of those. But no one I knew had a car of their very own.

And I knew that if Coy gave me that car, I couldn't take it home. Maybe not even after we were married, for fear my father would have my brothers ruin it.

Dad could be mean. I knew that. I'd seen it.

It seemed like the men in my family and the men in Coy's had a few things in common. That was one reason why I found Coy to be so special—he didn't seem to have a mean bone in his entire body.

His mother had been my third-grade teacher, and from what I remembered, she was very nice. I figured he must take after her. But she wasn't standing up for her son when it came to his future, which I found not so nice.

I began walking once more, as Coy had been inside the salesman's office for quite some time. Not in any hurry to get back home, I walked at a slow pace, wondering why a woman as nice as Mrs. Gentry would be onboard with Operation Keep Lila and Coy Apart.

I'd heard about her car accident. And I knew she'd be in a wheelchair for quite some time. Two of the bones in her lower back were broken. I was sure that her injuries had something to do with why she wasn't defending her son and his right to choose who he dated.

A car came barreling down the street, horn honking and tires squealing as it came to a stop right next to me. "Lila!" Janine, my best friend, shouted from the passenger side of the car her boyfriend, Dave, was driving. "There you are! Your father is looking for you. One of your little brothers told him that he was looking in your purse and found lots of money. He's sure you've been seeing that Gentry guy that he told you to stay away from. He's pissed, too. And he's out driving around, looking for you."

Clutching my purse, I didn't know what to do. "Thanks,

Janine. I've gotta go do something real quick. Don't tell anyone that you saw me. Please."

"I won't. Geeze, you should know that you can trust me—I'm your best friend, Lila." She rolled her eyes as if she couldn't believe how I'd been hiding things from her. "What kind of friend do you think I am?"

"A good one. And I'll tell you more later on. Right now, I've gotta get someplace." I took off running back the way I'd come. I had to get the money back to Coy, or my father would surely take it from me. And he would surely look through my purse, so I had to give Coy the marriage license to hold on to as well.

Coy was still inside when I got to the used car lot. So I got into his truck and squished myself into the floor so that no one would see me if they drove by. I wasn't sure if anyone in my family knew what kind of car Coy drove, so I was still freaking out that I might be found before I could give everything to Coy. They were the most important things in the world to us at that time—I couldn't let him down by letting my father get a hold of them.

When I heard Coy's voice, I finally felt okay. "I'll be back in three days to pick it up. Make sure it's all detailed for me."

"Will do, sir. It's been nice doing business with you," the salesman called out.

As soon as Coy opened the driver's side door, he saw me, and his blue eyes flew wide. "Hey." He got into the truck as if he wasn't worried about why I was hiding on the floor. "So, what's up?"

"One of my nosy brothers must've been snooping in my purse last night and saw the money you gave me. He told my father, and now my father is searching for me."

"And who told you this?" he started the truck and started driving away.

"One of my best friends saw me walking and told me." I took my wallet out of my purse and placed it on the seat. "Here, take

59

this and hide it." I got the marriage license too and put it on the seat next to my wallet. "And this too. If he finds it, he'll rip it up and do only God knows what to me."

"This isn't good at all." He sped up as his dark brows furrowed. "I hate this."

"Me too." I didn't know what else to do, though. "What will I tell my father when he finds no money?"

"Tell him that it wasn't real money, just some play money that you got from the dime store to play poker with your friends. And get that friend of yours to verify the story too. Tell her to say that you guys have been playing for a couple of weeks, and that's why you had it."

He parked the truck. "I'm going to run into the dime store now and get you some of that fake money to make the story sound legit."

At that moment, I thought Coy was the smartest man on the planet. "I love you and your amazing brain."

"I love you too, and soon we'll be laughing about all of this." He left me with a grin, and I began to feel that everything was going to be fine. With Coy on my side, nothing could go wrong.

As I waited for him to come back, I tried to figure out how to become the best actress I could possibly become when I ran into my father.

A half-hour later, I had the play money in a wallet Coy had picked up at the dime store and was walking back home. That was when my father pulled up next to me, and my three brothers got out of the car, yanking my purse off my shoulder. "Hey, what the hell are you doing?" I shouted as if I had no idea.

Tony tossed the purse into the car to my father, who sat behind the steering wheel. "Check it, Dad. You'll see. Her wallet is full of money."

"What?" I laughed as I shook my head. "You went through my purse?"

"Yes, and don't even try to lie, Lila!" Tony shouted at me.

My father had already gotten into my purse and had the fake money in his hand. "What's this shit?"

"Play money, Dad," I said. "Me and some of my friends have been playing poker with fake money."

My father shoved the money back into my purse, then threw it out of the passenger window. "Get back in the car, you idiots."

"So, can I get an apology?" I asked, knowing damn well that none would be given.

They sped off as my father cussed like a sailor, and I had a smile on my face that would not quit.

That worked like a charm.

FIONA

November 14th, 1970 – Carthage, Texas – Local Hospital

Cradling my son in my arms, I finally knew what love felt like. "Coy Marcus Gentry."

"Coy *Collin* Gentry," my husband said as he sat down on the hospital bed next to me.

I wasn't sure I wanted my son to have the same name as his father, even if it was only a middle name. He already had the bad luck of having his last name. "Why don't you like Marcus?"

"Why do you like that name?" He picked up the paper and pen off the tray. "We've got to fill this out for the birth certificate. I'll write down our names as the parents while you think about what it means to me that my son carries my name."

"He is a Gentry, you know." And that was already one strike against the poor boy.

Living with Collin's parents had been an eye-opener for me. He was a carbon-copy of his father. And the worst part of that was that Collin didn't act like his father because he looked up to him; he did it because he was terrified of the man.

I'd never heard anyone speak to another human being the way Collin's father did to him when he was disappointed in something he'd done. And I didn't want Collin to treat our son that way.

As it was, we were already meeting his father's wishes by naming our son Coy, which was Collin's father's middle name. And now Collin wanted me to saddle the kid with two names that were associated with hard asses. I just wasn't sure I wanted to do that to my son.

"It would make my father happy, you know." And that was all he had to say to me.

I wasn't about to bring down the buckets of guilt his father would rain down on him if he were to disappoint him. "Fine. Coy Collin it is then."

He hurried to write it down on the paper before I changed my mind. "Good."

"The next boy gets named after *my* father." I had to stand up for myself, at least a little. "And I get to pick all the girl names too."

"Then I get to pick all the boy names, after the second one."

"It's a deal." I looked down at the tiny face of my son and smiled. "He's so adorable."

"He's small though." He put his huge hand on top of our son's little head, dwarfing it. "See. He's a runt."

My ire sped to the surface. "He's not a runt. Seven pounds and nine ounces is average. Were you thinking he'd come out full-grown?"

"No." He laughed as he backed away from me. "I just thought, seeing as he's *my son,* he'd come out bigger." He gestured to his large stature. "I'm six-three you know. And Mom said I weighed ten pounds when I was born."

"Well, your mother is a lot bigger than me. I'm glad he didn't weigh that much. I can't imagine having to give birth to a baby that size."

Shrugging, he said, "Yeah, it would've probably ripped up a frail woman like you anyway. I guess it's best that he came out small."

"He's not small. He's perfectly average." I saw nothing wrong with being average.

"Anyway, now that you've had him, you know there will be no going back to work for you, right?" He'd been on me to quit my teaching job at the elementary school since the day he found out I was pregnant. But I wasn't about to let down all the kids in my class by dumping them. They would've to spend the remainder of the year being taught by a substitute.

Thankfully, I'd trained a student teacher to take over for me for when I had the baby. She was nice, and the kids liked her. And if I wanted to stay home with the baby, she'd make a suitable replacement. But I wasn't sure that I wanted to do that yet.

"We'll see about that later on when he's a bit older. I don't want to make any big decisions right now. I just want to look at my adorable baby and fall in love with him." I couldn't stop looking at my perfect little angel.

I saw my husband rolling his eyes before he left with the paperwork to give them to the nurse. He was in a huge rush to turn them in. "I'll be right back. You want anything? A soda pop or something?"

"No, thank you." I was as content as I could be with my baby in my arms. "Momma loves you."

He wrapped his tiny hand around my pinky, holding it tightly. I felt it was his way of telling me that he loved me too. I'd never been so happy in my entire life.

I heard a knock on the doorframe and was startled to see the first doctor I'd gone to all those months ago when I thought I might have been pregnant. "Hi there. I saw your name on the door and thought I'd stop by to see how you two are doing?"

I could feel my cheeks stained pink with a blush. I was a bit embarrassed that I'd just stopped going to him cold turkey. But Collin had been so upset by what he'd done that I didn't want to push it. "Oh, Doctor Nelson, thanks for stopping by. We're both doing very well."

He came to the side of the bed to look at my son. "He's a nice-looking boy, Fiona. I was just in the hospital checking on a patient who delivered yesterday. When I saw your name on the chart out there, I had to stop by. I hope that's okay with you."

I had to offer him a reason why I stopped coming to him. "I'm sorry about switching doctors. I decided I wanted a female doctor instead. You must understand, I'm sure."

"Sure I do. A lot of first-time mothers opt for a female doctor. It's a hard time for them, and it helps them feel better about everything. I totally get it. But keep me in mind for your next baby. I'm sure now that you've been through everything, you're much more at ease with all the things that go on when you're pregnant."

"Yes, I am. I'll keep you in mind when we have our next one." It was lie; Collin would never agree with me ever going back to see him.

He looked over his shoulder, then back at me. "Did you and your husband work out that little problem you were having?"

"We did." We hadn't, but I wasn't about to tell him that. "Thanks for all your help."

"Not a problem." He patted me on the shoulder. "You know, back in the old days, women came to doctors all the time with what they called hysteria back then. The ladies were aggravated and snapping at their husbands and families, and no one could figure out why. The story goes that a doctor during that time began asking intimate questions, and he found that all of these ladies who were being treated for hysteria had one thing in common."

I felt my cheeks heating up as I blushed. "They didn't have orgasms."

"Yep. So, this doctor began to manually stimulate the clitoris of each one of his female patients who'd been diagnosed with hysteria. He ended up with so many patients seeking his unique treatment method that he ended up building a vibrating machine to make his job easier and not so hard on the fingers. Plus, it sped up the climax, that way, he could see more patients."

"And I bet he ended up selling his machines to his patients so they could tend to themselves at home."

"He did, and now the world is a much better place." He laughed, and then his eyes cut to one side as my husband's large frame filled the doorway. "And this must be Mr. Gentry." He walked towards him with his hand extended. "Hello, I'm Doctor Nelson."

As Collin shook the man's hand, his eyes moved to me. "Is that so?"

"He saw my name on the chart and stopped by to see how the baby and I are doing." My heart sped up as I knew Collin had put two and two together.

"So, you were my wife's first doctor then," Collin said. "The one who told her that she was going to be a mother for the first time."

I prayed my husband would stay in control of his jealousy and his temper. "Honey, did you get me that soda I asked for?" I knew I'd turned down his offer, but I had to do something to separate the two of them.

"You said you didn't want one." He looked at me with a furrowed brow.

"You must've misheard me, dear. I would really like one. I'm so thirsty, and I'm tired of drinking water."

"I can grab you one if you'd like," the doctor offered. "It's no trouble at all."

"I'll get it." Collin stepped back, and the doctor was finally able to walk out the door. "See you, doc. And I'll be right back with the soda, Fiona."

"Bye now," the doctor said as he left us.

I let out a long sigh of relief as they both left. "What a fiasco that almost was, my son. What a fiasco indeed."

Later that night, after Collin had gone home to sleep, a woman wearing an apron with red stripes came to my room. She wheeled in a cart with magazines on top of it. "Candy striper. Would you like anything to read?" Her long dark hair was pulled back into a ponytail, and her caramel lips were curved into a smile.

The baby lay sleeping in his tiny bassinet, as the nurse hadn't come back for him yet after I'd finished feeding him. The young woman pushed the cart next to me, then went to stand over the bassinet.

"He's a cutie, isn't he?" I picked up a couple of magazines, opting for entertainment over education.

"Yes, he is." She ran her hand over my sleeping son's head. "He's precious."

"I agree. He's our first child. Are you married?" I flipped open the latest copy of Reader's Digest.

"No." She let out a long sigh as she gazed at my son. "And I don't have any babies of my own." She looked at me out of the corner of her eye. "You said he's your first child. Does that mean you plan on having more?"

"Oh, yes. My husband and I want as many children as the good Lord sees fit to give us." As I moved to resituate myself, the discomfort of recently having a baby was brought back to my attention. "But I think I'll give it a year or so before I try to get pregnant again. Not an easy thing, childbirth. I think I'll need time to forget the pain before I purposely put another bun in my oven."

"And your husband agrees with that?" She turned to face me, placing her hands on the cart.

"This is *my* body. I make the decisions about when I get pregnant." I held up the three magazines I'd picked out. "Thanks for these. I'm sure to be entertained now."

The sound of voices coming from the hallway made her jerk

her head to look at the door. "I should get going. There are more mothers who need something to read."

I looked at her apron and saw no nametag. All the other candy stripers I'd seen around the hospital had nametags. "I think you lost your nametag, miss."

A frown turned her mouth into a horseshoe. "Oh, yeah. Well, I'd better backtrack to see where it came off. Congratulations on the baby. He looks like a fine boy."

"Thank you."

"You know, you look to be around my age. My husband and I are the same age. Are you from Carthage?"

She nodded. "Born and raised."

"You most likely went to school with my husband, Collin Gentry." I watched as she ducked her head, eyes on the floor.

"Yes, we did go to school together. He and his father employed some of my brothers from time to time. I even did a short stint as a maid out at the ranch." She pushed the cart towards the door, hesitating for a moment before leaving.

I took the chance to say, "Tell me your name, and I'll tell my husband that I met you. He'll get a kick out of that, I'm sure."

"Oh, sorry, gotta go." And with that, she left.

I could hear the sound of the cart's squeaky wheels going fast down the long hallway. It sounded as if she was in a hurry, passing in front of all the other rooms instead of stopping as she'd said she was going to.

Something about her felt odd. I couldn't quite put my finger on it, but there was something about the young woman that bothered me.

But then again, she may have just been embarrassed for telling me she'd been a maid at the ranch I now lived at. The haves and have-nots of the small town didn't often speak to one another. Not that I was like that. I'd talk to and befriend anyone.

Collin and his mother and father weren't like me, though.

They only associated themselves with the people they deemed to be on their level in society, which I found snobbish. The young woman must've been ashamed she'd told me about her past as a maid.

Poor girl.

❧ 12 ❧

COLLIN

On the day my son turned six weeks, I made my last visit to Hilda. Only, she had no idea this would be the last time we would see each other.

Pulling into the drive, I found her coming to the door, opening it to welcome me inside. "Long time no see, stranger."

It had been a few months since I'd come to her. Becoming a father had hit me hard, even before my son was born. I had tremendous responsibilities now. And I could no longer tempt fate by messing around with Hilda.

The time had come to let her go.

The majority of my heart now lay in the palm of my infant son's tiny hands. But there was still a little piece that belonged only to Hilda. So, what I had to tell her was going to hurt me badly.

Stepping inside the home—the last time I'd ever do that—I took a look around. She had always kept it very neat and tidy, not a speck of dust to be found. "I'm glad you've taken good care of your home, even in my absence."

"I did not know whether you might show up or not." She closed the door, then walked towards the kitchen. "Would you care for a glass of iced tea? I'm not used to seeing you in the light of day. I'm not sure how to act."

Her unique scent filled my nostrils, and I inhaled it deep into my lungs, desperate to keep a part of her with me forever. "I don't want anything to drink. This isn't going to be the most pleasant visit, Hilda."

Walking back into the living room, she took a seat, a grim expression on her face. "You found out what I did, didn't you?"

I had no idea what she was talking about, but I acted as if I did. If she'd done something that might get me into trouble, I needed to know. "I want *you* to admit out loud what you did."

"It's true. I went to the hospital after your son was born. I saw him—and I saw her." She clasped her hands in her lap as if to prepare herself for my wrath.

She went to see Coy and Fiona?

"Tell me what you said." I kept my chin up high, acting as if I already knew everything—which I certainly did not.

"I didn't tell her my name. But I did tell her that I worked for a short time as a maid at the ranch, and I told her that I went to school with you. But that's all I said." Her eyes held the floor as she waited for me to dole out her punishment.

But there wouldn't be one. "It sounds as if no harm was done." Fiona hadn't said a word to me about their interaction, so I knew there wasn't anything to worry about. "Thank you for being honest with me."

Wide eyes met mine—she looked utterly confused. "I thought that's why you weren't coming to see me. I mean, not for the months before his birth, but afterward. I thought you were so angry with me that you kept yourself away for my own protection."

"No, that's not why I stayed away." I continued to keep my distance from her, pacing on the other side of the living room. I was as far away as I could get from her without leaving the room.

"So why did you?" She couldn't pull her eyes off of me. Eyes that were full of worry and concern. "You're making me nervous, Collin."

I faced her, squaring my shoulders as I prepared myself. "Becoming a father has changed me in ways I hadn't expected. Well, that's not entirely true. I had the feeling that I would begin thinking of my life differently than I had before. There's more I can lose now."

"No one has found out about us in all these years, and *now* you're getting worried?" She stood up but kept her distance from me. "Why now? And what do you think anyone would if we were found out? Take your son away? Not likely."

"My father can still throw me out, Hilda. And he can let my wife and son stay on at the ranch, without me. Believe me, I've thought this through. I don't want to lose you. But I really have no choice. It's my *son* I'm talking about here. My *blood*."

"You can't do this to me. You took everything away from me —and my only consolation was having you. And not even all the time or all to myself either."

"We did talk about the fact that I would have to marry someone else one day and that I would be expected to have a family too. I *am* expected to provide more heirs for the ranch, and you know that." I couldn't believe how she'd conveniently scrubbed that off from her memory bank.

"You talk like you're some sort of royal or something. You're just ranchers, Collin. Who the hell cares who ends up with that damn ranch after you and your father are dead?" She threw her hands into the air. "I can't believe you would do this to me over that godforsaken piece of land."

"This is about my son, not the ranch." I hadn't expected her to act this way. I had expected lots of crying and pleading. But arguing with me wasn't something I'd thought Hilda would ever do. For as long as I'd known her, she'd worshipped me.

As intoxicating as that had always been, I had to end what we had. But I couldn't let her think she was on her own, and I wasn't exactly abandoning her, leaving her to figure out how to make money after I'd taken care of her for the last few years. "Hilda, I've already bought you a home in Shreveport, Louisiana."

She plopped down on the couch. I hadn't ever seen her look this way. She had an agitated air about her, and for once, it seemed like pleasing me was the furthest thing on her mind. "I need you to tell me what the hell you're doing. I'm desperately trying to understand why you would buy me a home in Shreveport when all of my family is here in Carthage. Am I to live in solitude? And for what? So you can have your family and forget I ever existed?" She made it sound so selfish.

My son needed me to do this. "Do you think this isn't hurting me? Killing me? Because it is. I—I" I'd never said the words out loud to her. But she needed to know how I felt. "I love you, Hilda Stevens. But I also love my son. And I hate to say this to you, but I love him more than I love myself. I have to do right by him."

"You should see things the right way. I've done your bidding for my own reasons. Reasons you could never understand, and I will never explain to you. But you need to know that I know you have never loved me. Nor have ever I loved you. We've *needed* each other. We've *used* each other. And that is all." She nodded. "What I don't understand is why I have to leave town and move to another state." Her hands covered her face as she began crying softly. "I don't want to lose you. I don't want to lose us. I can't do the things we do together with anyone else."

My heart ached, and my arms itched to hold her in them. But that would only make what I had to do harder. "Hilda, I've bought you a decent home. And I've already gone up there and opened a bank account. The checks will be mailed to you at your new place. The account is in your name only. But I'll make weekly deposits in the same amount I do for you now."

"So this is it then." She pulled her hands away from her face, which was red and tearstained. "You'll take care of me until you die, and *I* will die alone."

I didn't want to think about death. "I don't know what the future holds, and you don't either. Let's not think that far down the road."

"You and your *wife*," she said the word as if it had thorns that cut her tongue as she spoke, "will have many children, according to her. And your children will keep you away from me. *Always!*"

What could I possibly say? She wasn't wrong. Not that I could tell her that. "Look, we don't know what the future holds. My father won't live forever."

"And after he dies, there will be your mother to keep happy. After she dies, you will have to keep your wife happy. It will *never* end. You and I will never be. Not ever! You're a coward, Collin Gentry. A coward and a liar."

I was stunned by her anger. "Hilda, please try to understand. I'm going to take care of you, no matter what." I'd never seen these expressions on her face before, and it made more uneasiness creep up inside of me.

"I don't care about a house or money if it means we will never be together. Death may be better than not having you anymore." Her chest rose and fell noticeably as she took several deep breaths.

"Watch what you say to me." I wasn't about to allow her to bully me with threats of suicide. "You *will* go to the home I bought for you. This one has already been sold. You'll be moving out today. I hired movers to pack your things and take them to the new place. You're to get into your car and follow them." I reached into my pocket and took out the set of house keys, then tossed them onto the coffee table. "Those are the keys to your new place. It's much nicer than this one. So what do you say?"

"You expect me to thank you?" Her body shook as if she was in shock. "You expect me to simply do whatever you say?"

"I do." I'd made things so easy for her ever since I'd come back from college. "I've given you a home of your own and that new car that's parked in the garage. I've given you thousands and thousands of dollars, and I pay all of your bills. I expect you to do as I say."

"And if I don't, then you'll cut me off?" She stood, then turned her back to me as if she could no longer stand to look at me.

"Yes." I would have no choice but to cut her off if she refused my very generous offer. "Don't make me do that. Just take the new house and the money. And we'll see what the future holds."

"I know what it will hold." She turned to me, tears freely cascading down her reddened cheeks. "You will live a happy life with your kids and your wife, and I will live a lonely existence with no one."

"You have my permission—" I had to stop and swallow as a knot formed in my throat. The idea of Hilda being with another man made me sick. But I had to stop being so goddamned selfish. "I'm sorry. As you can see, this isn't easy for me, Hilda. You have my permission to find another man."

"How *heroic* of you, Collin," sarcasm dripped off her tongue with words she did not truly mean. "May you live the life you deserve and have the family you deserve. You no longer need to keep me in your mind since I'm nothing but a taboo to you and your family."

Her words hurt, but hearing them gave way for some relief—and a little hope. Hope that I might finally cast off this dark obsession I had with her. That I could resist my dark desires—so long as she was far away from me.

❧ 13 ❧

FIONA

1976 – Dallas, Texas – All-Boys Boarding School

It seemed like a punishment to me. Since being blessed with Coy's birth, we hadn't had another child. And Collin put the blame squarely on my shoulders. Now he was sending our only child—six-year-old Coy—away to boarding school. Even if he wouldn't admit it, I knew he was doing it to punish me for what he thought were my failings.

Coy sat in the backseat of our car, his eyes wide as he looked out the window at the tall buildings in downtown Dallas. "This isn't like home, Daddy."

"It's still a good place, son. You'll really love it here. And you'll have lots of boys your own age to play with. You don't have anyone to play with at home," Collin looked at me, "since you don't have any brothers or sisters."

"He made friends in kindergarten last year when he went," I pointed out. "And he'd be in class with most of them this year too. This isn't necessary, Collin."

"I want my son to get a good education, and Carthage public schools just won't cut it." That was one of the many great reasons —or so he said—why our son had to leave home. And he had his father's backing him up, so it seemed that things were set in stone. "I grew up as an only child, Fiona. It was a lonely existence, and I don't want that for Coy."

"You seem to forget that I'm an only child too, Collin. I had lots of friends and was perfectly happy. Coy is a lot like me. He makes friends easily."

Collin didn't make friends easily, so he had none. But Coy wasn't his father. He was much more like me. Unfortunately, my husband wouldn't see that in our son.

"What did I tell you about talking about this in front of him?" he growled at me.

"Daddy, I don't want to leave home to go to school. I can play with my friends at my old school. I'll miss you all so much. Please don't make me go," Coy pleaded.

Collin glared at me as if this was all my fault. "See what you've done. Fix it, Fiona. Fix it right now."

I knew my husband wasn't going to bend on this. Trying my best not to roll my eyes, I turned in my seat to look at Coy. "You know, maybe Daddy's right. Maybe this *will* be a good thing for you. It will be like having lots of brothers. That'll be nice. Don't you think so?"

He shook his head as his lower lip drooped. "No."

Collin had said we'd pick up Coy for the holidays, but looking at my sweet boy's sad face, I made an executive decision at the last minute. "I tell you what, Coy. We will pick you up every Friday once school is out, and you can stay with us, at home, until Sunday evening. We'll have to bring you back Sunday night, but at least you'll see us every single week. That's three days out of seven that you'll be with us."

"We never agreed to that," Collin grumbled. "I'm not even sure that's something I can do."

"I can go and bring him back if you're too busy. I do drive, you know. I have my own car." I'd gone back to work, teaching at the elementary school last year when Coy started kindergarten. And I would be working that school year too. I wouldn't even have to ask him for money to go get our son. "It's not a problem for me. I want to see him each week."

"I want that too, Daddy. Please, let her," Coy whimpered.

I wasn't about to let Collin make the decision. I'd already made it. "I *will* come to get you on Fridays, son. You'll be with us Friday nights, all day and night on Saturdays, and all day on Sundays too. And then there are all the holidays you'll get to come home for. It won't be so bad, you'll see."

Collin didn't like it when I made decisions. He didn't like the fact that I decided to go back to work. He didn't like when I had any independence at all. But I did it anyway. Collin had to learn that he wasn't in charge of me. And he needed to learn that he wasn't in complete charge of our son either.

I saw his knuckles turning white as he clutched the steering wheel, trying not to blow up at me in front of our son. "Fine, Fiona. Have it your way."

Smiling at Coy, I was happy when he smiled back at me. "Thanks, Momma. I feel better now."

It wasn't everything I wanted—what I wanted most was Coy at home with us. But at least I would have him there more than I had thought I would.

When we arrived at the boarding school, I felt myself falling apart. Knowing that I couldn't do that in front of Coy, I sucked it up as we got out of the car in the parking lot of the huge building.

"This place is enormous. So much bigger than the pictures on the pamphlet." I took Coy's little hand in mine. "But it's really nice looking. Isn't it, son?"

"It's really big, Momma. What if I get lost?"

Collin came up on Coy's other side. "You won't get lost. There will be lots of other boys around, and there're teachers here too. There's nothing to worry about."

Coy looked up at his father. "Why didn't you go to a school like this, Daddy?"

"I wish I had gone to a school like this, Coy. But my parents didn't know there were such things as this when I was a kid. I think you're incredibly lucky to have a father who found this place for you." Collin shot a look at me that told me he had no intention of being the bad guy. "I'm doing this for you because I love you, son. And I want what's best for you."

He could spout that all he wanted. I knew better than that, though he'd never admit it. No matter how many times I'd asked him if he was angry with me for not being able to have more children, he would always tell me that it wasn't an issue.

Collin said the right things. He did tell me that he didn't think it was my fault. But he didn't say that it might be him who was to blame either.

The lack of children was a subject he didn't like talking about. To him, it was what it was, and there was nothing anyone could do about it. But from time to time, I would catch him looking at me with pure disgust, and I knew why that was—even if he wouldn't admit it.

Collin's mother and father only had one child as well. It wasn't planned that way; it had just happened that way. I had the feeling that a low sperm count was to blame in both my husband and his father.

I was also an only child, but my parents had had more of a say in that. My mother had high blood pressure, and when she'd been pregnant with me, it had nearly killed her. So, right after birth, the doctor gave her a tubal ligation to prevent any more pregnancies.

Much like his father, Collin didn't like to take the blame for anything. If a woman could be blamed, then she was. I'd watched Collin's father blame his wife for things that she'd never done, time and time again.

Collin tried to do that with me, but I wouldn't accept the blame the way his mother did. I wasn't as weak-willed as his mother. It was obvious that Collin hadn't thought I would be so strong-willed when he'd asked me to marry him. He'd often

mumble underneath his breath that he'd married me too soon—
that he hadn't gotten a chance to get to know the real me.

But when I'd ask him what he said, he'd say, "Nothing." And
that would be it.

I knew what I'd heard, though. And I knew sending our son
away was only done to hurt me.

But I wouldn't let him. As hard as he might try, Collin Gentry
would never break me.

14

COLLIN

May 1988 – Carthage, Texas

Standing in the middle of the dance floor at the American Legion in Carthage, I privately congratulated myself. I'd truly outdone myself. Putting together a high school graduation party for Coy all by myself had been quite the undertaking.

Fiona hadn't been able to help since she'd been injured in a car wreck a few weeks before the big event. Now she was in a wheelchair. She'd broken both her legs and had fractures in her two lower vertebrae. The wreck had taken its toll on her body, which I'd always thought had been on the frailer side anyway. The doctors had said that she would make a full recovery, but it could take a year or longer before that occurred.

Without Fiona to help me, I'd had to do it all—decorations, refreshments, guest list. I'd invited the entire senior class from the local high school too. That way, Coy could reconnect with the kids he'd gone to kindergarten with.

Now that he'd be living back at the ranch, working for me until it was time for him to head off to college in the fall, I wanted him to think of Carthage as his home.

Coy hadn't hung out with any of his old friends when he came home to visit. His mother monopolized his time too much for him to be able to spend it with anyone outside our little family circle. But that would end now. I'd make her back off of him and let him become the man he now was at eighteen years old.

It wouldn't be hard to do either, since she wasn't in the best of health. Her strong will had taken a hard hit with her injuries. Not only was she unable to take physical care of herself, but she also wasn't able to work and wouldn't be able to until next year. And that was only if everything healed as it should.

I'd hired a full-time nurse to tend to Fiona. Not that it made her happy. She hated being so dependent on others. Her mood wasn't often happy anymore.

The party would begin shortly, and when the doors opened, I turned to see who was coming in. It was my parents, followed by my wife and son. Coy pushed his mother's wheelchair, both wearing big smiles as they looked at what I'd done.

I opened my arms to gesture at the decorations. "So, did Dad do good by you, son?"

"I'll say." He looked all over the place. "Dad, this is amazing."

Fiona couldn't wipe the smile off her face. "Collin, I can't believe you did this all by yourself."

"I am a capable man." Walking to the table filled with drinks, I filled a small cup with fruit punch and took it to my wife. "Try this out."

"Is it spiked?" she asked with knowing eyes. "Because I've just taken some pain meds so I could come out here. If I mix alcohol with them, I might end up dead."

My father patted her on the shoulder. "Now, now, Fiona, he wouldn't put alcohol in something meant for a bunch of underage kids, you know."

She still looked at me to make sure of that. I laughed. "Fiona, seriously, do you think I want to tend to a bunch of drunk teenagers?"

With a nod, she took a sip. "You would never want to deal with that."

Coy went to look around at every single thing in the hall, his blue eyes full of excitement. He had my dark hair, my tall height, and my muscular build, but he had his mother's blue eyes. I was sure that if he'd gone to a high school with girls instead of the all-boys boarding school we'd sent him to, he would've had to beat the girls off with a stick.

The stage was set with instruments for the band that would be starting soon. "You got a live band?" he asked.

"I did." I couldn't have wiped the smile off my face if I'd wanted to.

"Wow, Dad!" He jumped up and clicked the heels of his cowboy boots. "Yee-haw! A real band!"

Not much later, the band came in, and people started showing up. Since I hadn't done much in the community, I wasn't sure about the kind of turnout we'd get for the party. But the live band and free food and drinks had them coming in droves.

Before we knew it, the dance floor was crowded, and everyone was laughing and having an excellent time. Coy had no trouble making friends, either. Many of the kids who he'd gone to kindergarten with recognized him immediately.

I sat at the family table with my wife and parents as we watched Coy have the time of his life. I leaned over to my wife. "He's doing great, isn't he?"

"He is," she agreed. "I guess going off to boarding school was good for him after all."

I couldn't believe she was finally agreeing with me on that. "And going off to college will have him coming back home with even more enthusiasm for life." Our son had such a love for life; it defied my imagination.

His heart was huge, too. He loved his grandparents, me, and his mother with all his heart. I was sure that he didn't know how to love any other way. And I hoped that the girl he ended up falling in love with would give him back what he had to give to her.

Coy was everything I could never be. And I had his mother to thank for that. God knows he didn't get his affinity for goodness and love from me or my side of the family.

I knew our reputation in town was that of a bunch of hardasses. Neither my father nor I put up with anything. If we ordered two-thousand bales of hay, there better be that many in the hay barn when they were through delivering it. We'd count each bale, and if it came up short, there was hell to pay.

A Gentry wouldn't be cheated on.

Tonight though, things were different. The Gentry family had put on a party for the whole town, and they'd come out to enjoy it. I knew why, too.

My wife had gained a good reputation as a teacher in town. She'd taught most of the graduating class at some time or another. She'd been a third-grade teacher, and she'd also taught fifth grade for the last few years, before her accident. She'd been teaching before Coy was even born, so she was all smiles as some of her old students waved at her.

It was because of her that we were able to have a successful party. Fiona was our key to acceptance in the town because no one cared for me or my father. Not that either of us cared. But everyone liked Fiona.

As the evening progressed, I saw Coy dancing with the same girl for at least ten songs. They swayed slowly, holding each other while talking.

The girl had dark eyes and silky dark hair. She was a real beauty, with caramel-colored skin and more curves than most of the girls her age. I could see why my son seemed to have an interest in her.

Since I had no idea of the names of anyone there, I asked my wife, "Who is he dancing with?"

84

"That's Lila Stevens." She smiled. "She's a nice girl. I taught her in third grade. She's really turned into such a beauty."

My heart froze as I heard her last name. "Do you remember her parents' names?"

"I know her mother's name is Beth, but I can't remember her father's name…" she tapped her chin as she tried to remember.

I recalled something that Hilda had mentioned when I had told her about Fiona being pregnant. "Arthur?"

"Yes, that's it. Arthur and Beth Stevens." She looked around as if looking for them. "I don't see them here, though."

That's because Arthur would never come to a party I'm throwing.

Arthur was Hilda's brother. He was one year younger than her. She'd told me that it was such a coincidence that he and I were both going to become fathers in the same year.

The girl my son was dancing with, the same one he was making calf eyes at, was Hilda's niece. And that was not good.

My father sat on Fiona's other side, and he'd overheard everything we'd said. He looked at me with one cocked brow as if telling me that I knew what I had to do.

I sat there, though, not wanting to move, not wanting to tell my son what I knew I had to.

In all the years that the Stevens family had lived in Carthage, they'd never pulled themselves out of the gutter. They were all just as poor as they'd always been. Most of them didn't even have high school diplomas, and none of them had college degrees.

A part of me thought that Coy could have a little summer fling with the girl, then he'd go off to college and find a real woman to marry and bring home.

Another part of me thought that he might fall in love with the girl and want to take her with him to college. I'd wanted to do that with Hilda. I'd wanted to pay her way through college. I'd wanted to bring her up to our level, so my father would finally accept her.

But I didn't handle the money at that time, so it was impossible to do what I wanted. And my father had made sure that I understood I was to leave Hilda behind, to keep her hidden right where she was.

The night before I'd left for college, my father had come into my bedroom. I'd had no idea that he knew about me and Hilda. I'd thought I'd successfully kept it a secret from everyone.

But my father had found out somehow, and he'd woken me up with a smack of a leather belt on my bare back. "Get up!"

"Ow!" I'd jumped out of bed, wearing nothing but underwear. "What's that for?"

"You thought I'd never catch on. You thought you could get away with it." Another strike of the belt had my cheek burning like fire after he struck me in the face.

"Dad, I've got my first day of classes tomorrow. Please!"

He'd hit me in the stomach next. "I will beat the flesh off of your bones, boy. You knew you were doing wrong when you did it—fucking that piece of trash, that whore, from that good for nothing family. I know you knew better than that. That's why you've been hiding it from me for so long. So, tell me what I have to hear, or I won't stop beating your ass before you're laying on the floor."

He would've done it too. He'd done it before. "I'll stop seeing her. I swear to you that I'll stop."

I'd gotten ten more lashes before he stopped, after I'd begged and begged for him to please quit beating me. I wasn't far from passing out when he left the room, leaving me with one last threat. "If you ever see her again, I will disown you, and you will be out on the streets without a damn thing."

He wasn't the kind of man who made idle threats—I knew that I had to go off to college and leave Hilda behind. I was able to do that for four years. It was only when I came back home and married Fiona, only after I found her to be such a prude, that I was left with no other choice but to go back to Hilda.

My father hadn't ever figured me out. Although he'd never caught on to the affair I'd had with Hilda, he now knew my son was attracted to someone from her family. And that was not good.

The first chance I got to talk to Coy alone, I took it. He was walking to the bathroom when I caught up to him and pulled him through a side door. "Hey, son, you look like you're having a good time."

"Dad, I really am," he gushed. "Thank you so much for doing this for me. It's really amazing. Everyone keeps talking about how great this is and how cool it is of you for putting it all together." He smiled. "For once, it seems like the town people like you, Dad."

"Yeah, I'm not used to this." And now I knew it wouldn't last. "Son, I know you don't know this, but our family isn't one to rub elbows with those people in town who don't try to make something of themselves."

His eyes flashed with anger, just like his mother's sometimes did. "What's that supposed to mean?"

"The girl you've been dancing with—"

He cut me off. "She's great. I really like her, and she seems to like me too. I've already asked her if she'd go out with me tomorrow night. She said yes. I'm going to take her to Dallas to show her my old school, and then I will take her out to eat at that restaurant that's shaped like a sphere and rotates."

"You can't do that."

"I can." He merely shook his head, thinking he could make his own decisions.

"No, you can't."

He set his jaw, and I knew he wasn't going to be easy to sway. "Why not?"

"She doesn't come from a good family. She won't be accepted by your family. Do you see what I'm getting at here?"

"Mom will accept whoever I bring home." He puffed out his chest. "And you will too."

"No, I won't." I—above all people—knew how unfair I was being. But my father was still alive, and I didn't want him going into my son's bedroom one night and beating the shit out of him. "Just find another girl, son. That's all I'm saying. Find one who's going to college, the way you are. That's all I ask."

"How do you know that Lila isn't going to college?" He was so much like his mother. And that worried me.

"I don't." But I didn't know of even one member of that family who had gone to college. "Did you ask her about that?"

"I did. I told her how I was going to be going to Lubbock to go to Texas Tech, just like you and Mom have."

"And what did she say?" I thought if I could go back and tell my father that this girl was going to go to school in the fall might make it okay for Coy to see her.

"Well, she said that her parents don't have money to send her. But if they did, then she would go."

"See, she comes from a bad family. If she had a good family, they would have made it a priority to save money so their kids could go to college. I'm sorry. You have to find yourself another girl, son."

Cocking his head, he looked at me as if I were crazy. "Dad, I'm not going to find another girl. I'm going out with Lila, and that's that. Come out of the Stone Age, and join the rest of the world." And then he walked away from me.

Just like his fucking mother!

88

❧ 15 ❧

FIONA

The night of our son's high school graduation party had been going extremely well. Until Collin pulled Coy outside to talk to him. I found Coy coming back with a scowl on his face, and soon after, Collin came in looking the same way.

I had no idea what could've set the two of them off. When my husband came back and sat next to me, I asked, "What's going on?"

"Your son is too damn much like you, that's what's going on." He pulled off his cowboy hat and ran his hands over his hair as if he had a headache.

"I still don't understand."

He pointed at the dance floor, where our son was dancing again with Lila Stevens. "See. He's doing that just to spite me."

I was completely lost. "How's that?"

"I told him to move on to another girl. But he can't take an order to save his fucking life." He huffed and closed his eyes as if he couldn't stand watching his son having a nice time with someone.

"If you ask me, the boy was spared the belt, and it shows," Collin's father said.

"Why do you care who Coy is spending time with, Collin?" I

tried to ignore his father's remarks; the old man spoke like some ancient caveman most of the time.

"You wouldn't understand, Fiona. But the fact is that I told him he needs to find another girl to dance with, and he's clearly not doing it." His ears had turned as red as beets. I knew that meant he was angry.

But I still couldn't understand why. "Just let him dance with whomever he wants." Collin's controlling nature could get the best of him at times. And I hoped he wouldn't ruin our son's party.

"You'll never understand things in this town, Fiona. That girl is from the wrong side of town. The name Gentry means something here. I fully expect my son to protect the name the same way my grandfather and my father did. The way I did."

"I can't see how he's smudging the family name by dancing with that girl." This was just too much.

"I didn't get to do it, and neither will he," Collin said with such anger in his voice that it actually frightened me.

His words just confused me even more. "Was there some girl from here that you weren't allowed to see, Collin?"

"Never mind," he growled before getting up and leaving.

His parents followed a half-hour later, and I was left sitting alone at the table, wondering what the hell was happening. When Coy saw me sitting alone, he came to me. "Where has everyone gone?"

"Home, I suppose." I'd ridden with Coy but had assumed Collin would take me home. "I hate to put a damper on your evening, Coy, but it seems I'll need you to give me a ride home."

"Of course, Mom. No problem at all." He sighed and shoved his hands into his pockets. "Man, Dad's a real snob. I never knew how much until tonight."

"What did he say to you?" *I might finally get some answers.*

"He told me that I can't see Lila. He said she comes from a bad family."

"Oh, I see. And you must've told him that you will see her if you want—or something of that nature." My son was like me in many ways. I was proud of him for that.

"Yep." He rocked on his heels. "Mom, I just can't let him dictate my life. And I really can't let him tell me who I can and cannot date. Sorry, I just can't do that."

"I know you can't." I was the same way. "Well, I'll talk to him. Not that I have any control over him, but sometimes I can make him understand that he's not in control of everyone else."

"I would appreciate it if you did that for me. I don't want to argue with him. But I'm not about to stop seeing someone I like just because of their family or how much money they might or might not have. I honestly have no idea why Dad is so pissed off."

Collin's father's words about Coy being spared beatings came to mind. "I'm sure it has something to do with your grandfather, Coy. I'll do what I can to put a stop to this nonsense. But how about that ride home now? I'm exhausted and in need of more pain killers."

Coy took me home and got me into the house. "Mom, I'm gonna go back into town to get Lila. We're gonna hang out for a bit longer. It's only a little after midnight. I'll be home in a few hours."

"You be careful, son." I knew he hadn't dated anyone before, and that worried me. "You don't know anything about this girl, so guard your heart until you get to know her better. She's the first girl you've gone out with, you know."

"I know. That's why I want to talk with her some more. I'm not trying to rush anything. But I like her, Mom. I like her a lot."

"Don't mistake physical attraction for something more. You should be intellectually attracted to a girl too." I trusted Coy. He was a good boy. "Good night. Have fun. I'll see you tomorrow."

"Good night, Mom. I love you."

"I love you too."

I wheeled myself to the downstairs bedroom, which I'd

moved into after my accident. Having to have my nurse help me dress and undress and move from the wheelchair to the bed made it so that I had to have a separate bedroom from Collin. Waking him up wasn't an option.

The nurse's bedroom was right next to mine; she heard me as the floorboards creaked under the weight of my chair. "There you are. I bet you're in need of your pain medication."

"You are so right, Lucy. And I'd love to get out of this chair and into my cozy bed."

🕉️

THE NEXT MORNING, I WAS WOKEN UP BY MY HUSBAND, WHO wore an angry expression. "When did he finally come home?"

"Coy?" I pulled myself up to a sitting position, which made my back spasm as the brace around me slipped. "Ow!"

Collin hurried to help me, slipping the brace back into place and pulling the strings to tighten it back up. "You have to be careful."

"Well, you woke me up, and I'm out of sorts, Collin." I panted as my lower back throbbed. "Hand me the pain killers, please."

Moving quickly, he got me a pill and handed me the glass of water I always kept on the nightstand. "Here, take this."

It took me a few minutes before I could start thinking straight, and when I finally could, I asked, "What's your problem, Collin?"

He stood there with his arms crossed over his chest. "Our son needs to do as I tell him. Did he leave after he brought you home?"

"Yes, he did. He went back into town to spend some time with Lila. And you need to mind your own business." I wasn't about to side with my husband on something this stupid.

"I'm saving him from himself. You wouldn't understand. He listens to you. I need your help with this."

He was a fool if he thought for a second that I'd help him.

"Collin, you know that I don't feel as if myself, you, or your parents are above anyone else. Coy is not above that girl. There is no above. We are all just people. And we can date and even fall in love with anyone we damn well please, regardless of their color, bank account, or family background. So, what did the Stevens family ever do to the Gentry family that made them persona non grata?"

He closed his eyes as his face went a shade of red that I hadn't seen before. "Look, I had to follow my father's rules growing up, and so does everyone who lives in this house or on this ranch. If Coy wants to continue living here, he will have to listen to what I say. And he can't date anyone from that family or any family that my father deems beneath us."

"No." I wasn't going to be a part of this idiocy. "I won't back you or your father on this. It's against my moral code, Collin. And it sounds like it's against our son's as well. He's eighteen—a man now. And I'm proud of him for sticking up for what he believes in."

"You leave me no choice then. If you aren't with me, then you are against me. If you don't back me up on this or accept whatever I choose to do to Coy, then you can get out of this house."

"I'm at your mercy right now, and you know that. I can't work for maybe a whole year. How will I pay rent? How will I get around? How will I pay my nurse if you send me away?" My father had already passed away from a heart attack, and my mother's high blood pressure had gotten so severe that she had to live in a nursing home. I had no one to go to if he sent me away.

"Don't make me send you away then. I'm not saying that you have to make Coy do as I say because I know that might well be impossible. He is so much like you, after all." He didn't make it sound like a compliment. "But I do expect you to back whatever I say and whatever threats I make or go through with. I'm not doing it to hurt our son. I'm doing it to save him from himself."

"You were interested in someone from that family a long time ago, and your father didn't allow you to pursue it. I can see it in your eyes. Did he beat you over it?" I'd seen enough of the ugly side of the Gentry's to think otherwise.

"He did. You're right. And I learned to obey what he fucking said, too. Do you want that to happen to our son?"

"I wouldn't allow it, and I expect you not to allow it either." I hated being so incapacitated at a moment when I truly needed my strength.

"He won't do it when anyone is around. And we both know that Coy won't fight back. Plus, my father can disown me if I can't make my son protect the family name. He's told me before that if I don't do as he demands, he will leave this ranch to the state before giving it to me."

I knew Collin's father was a hard-ass—that he could even be cruel at times. But I had no idea he could be so downright evil and spiteful. It made me sick to think that I'd lived in the same home as a man who was capable of such atrocities.

"Collin, we should move out of this house. We should leave the ranch anyway. We can't allow that man to control us or our son. You have a degree and loads of experience. You can get a job as a ranch manager in no time. It's not nearly as much money as you have, but it's an honest living, and then no one can tell you how to live your life or how to treat your son."

"I can't do that. And believe me, you wouldn't want me if I left this ranch. Tell me what I need to hear from you, Fiona, or I'll pack your things and send you away this very day. I swear to you that I will do it."

My heart skipped a beat. I loved my son more than anything, but in this condition, what choice did I have?

I could only hope that one day, Coy would understand.

✵ 16 ✵
COY

July 1988 – Carthage, Texas

Driving home, I decided that I had to give my parents one more shot. I'd never been in an argument with either of them, and it occurred to me that I didn't know how to argue my point with them. But I had taken a debate class, so I knew how to argue.

As I walked into the house, I tried to make a list of pros that I could think of about me and Lila. There were a lot of them. And the only cons pertained to my family and hers.

My mother sat in her wheelchair alone in the living room, reading a book. She looked up at me with a smile as I came into the room. "There you are. You've been so busy this summer. Where've you been today?"

For a moment, I wanted to tell her the truth. But even if she didn't like the idea of me being with Lila, she would hate knowing that we'd gotten a marriage license and planned to get married in three days. Without her there.

So, I lied, "Just messing around with some of the guys I was in kindergarten with. You know, the ones I reconnected with at the party you guys so generously threw."

"That's nice." She put her book on the table next to her, giving me her full attention. "We're having chicken fried steak for dinner this evening. Your favorite."

"Good." I was hungry. I just hoped I would still be hungry after our conversation. "So, while Dad's not in the house, I want to talk to you about something."

Her jaw tightened right away, and she clasped her hands in her lap. "About what?"

I took a seat so that we were on the same level. "Mom, it's about Lila Stevens. I don't understand why we can't see each other."

She looked over her shoulder as if trying to make sure no one would hear us, then looked back at me. "Son, I know this isn't right. I'm not the kind of person who thinks anyone is any better than someone else. But I'm not your only parent. And your grandparents own this house and the ranch. Your father hasn't inherited it yet. And, frankly, I'm not one hundred percent sure he'd allow you to see Lila, even if he were in charge right now."

"But why?" I couldn't understand why my father had to take a stand on this.

"Your father was raised differently," she said. "His parents instilled their values in him, and they soaked in thoroughly. This ranch is everything to him and your grandfather. And they will do anything they deem necessary to make sure the next generations uphold their strict values. And these values make it so that any children of theirs have to hold themselves to the same standards as they do."

"Mom, come on." I knew she didn't think the way they did. "Can't you talk some sense into them?"

A weak smile curved her pale lips. "I have tried. But your father won't hear another word about that from me. He's made it clear that if I'm not with him, then I'm against him."

"Mom, you know that you can have your own opinion. And you know that your opinion matters." I didn't like seeing my mother like this. "Why are you backing him on this? You're a strong woman."

"But I am not independent—especially not right now. I rely on your father for everything. I am so sorry that my injuries are interfering with what you need right now. I truly am. But there is absolutely nothing that I can do about it." A tear ran down her cheek, and she quickly wiped it away. "Just do as he says, Coy. Don't make waves. There are more fish in the sea, I promise you that. And college is going to start in the fall, and you'll meet many young women from all over the place there. Women who are as energetic and educated as you. Women who you might be more compatible with."

"Mom, Lila and I are extremely compatible."

"I'm sure that you think that, Coy." She shook her head. "Lila is a small-town girl who probably hasn't ever been further away than Dallas. She's not going anywhere."

"So?" I had no idea why that would even matter. "I'm coming back here to this ranch after college, so I'm not going anywhere either. I'll eventually take over this ranch and live out the remainder of my life right here. What makes me any different from her?"

"You've gone to a better school than she has, for one. And you'll get a college degree that will make you even more well-rounded. When you come back for your first visit after being in college for a semester, you'll see that you've outgrown the likes of a small-town girl."

"I don't even believe that for a second." Sighing, I didn't know how to make her believe that I was in love with Lila. "Mom, we've been seeing each other in secret."

"I'm going to pretend that I did not hear that. And I don't want you to repeat it. I need you to stop seeing her. This is for your own good. You must trust me on this. Forget about her, let the future show you what it has in store for you. I met your father in college. I'd had a couple of boyfriends before him, but it was different when I met him. It could happen for you just like that too."

"Mom, I've found the one for me. I don't need to date anyone else to know that."

Shaking her head, she hissed, "Stop saying things like that. It makes it sound as if you've been spending time with her. Your father will see right through you. And you can't let him do that."

I had a strong feeling that she didn't believe anything she was saying—that there was another source behind all of this. "I think I'll go talk to Grampa."

All color drained from her face, and her mouth fell open. "No. Promise me that you won't do that. It would be unbelievably bad for you if you did that."

"The worst thing that anyone can do to me is take away my inheritance."

"You are wrong. You have no idea how wrong you are." She wrung her hands in her lap; it was obvious that I'd upset her. "Drop this, now. End things, now. I am pleading with you, Coy."

"Coy Collin," I said with disgust. "Named after the two most stubborn men I've ever met. Why do they refuse to understand that the heart wants what the heart wants? I can't have whoever *I* choose. I must take whoever *they* approve of." I looked at my mother, who was the epitome of a prim and proper wife. "Look at yourself. A college-educated woman who knows her place. Seems Dad picked you because you fit the role, Mom. Tell me how many times the word *love* has been said between you and my father."

"Coy, please stop," she whimpered, which was unlike her. "I didn't raise you to be cruel like this. You might be a man now, but you're still young. There's still a lot you don't know about how the world works—about how marriages work."

"I might be young, but I know what I want. I know I want a marriage with *love* at its heart. Not similar educations. Not playing a role. *Love,* Mom. *Love* is what makes the world go 'round. *Love* will see you through everything. Not being on the same financial tier. Not being on the same level." I had never felt more disgusted with my mother in my entire life. "You didn't stand up for me when I didn't want to be taken and left at boarding school when I was six, and you won't do it now either."

"I can't." She ran her hands over her injured legs. "I'm in no condition to fight a battle with your father. And to be perfectly honest, I don't think it would be worth it, in the end. She is the first girl you've ever kissed, and I think that's why you've formed this bond so quickly." She ran her hand over her face. "Life is too big to marry only for love. Life hits you hard at times, and you need a partner you can trust. If you listen to nothing else I tell you, at least listen to that. And you need to heed the advice of those who love you and have your best interests at heart. Which your father and I do. Son, I feel as if I made the decision to marry your father too soon. And I don't want to see you do something similar to what I did. Just wait before marrying this girl, please."

The sounds of my father's boots against the wooden floor echoed in the living room. Mom's eyes begged me not to say a word to him about what we'd talked about.

But I couldn't do what she wanted. "Dad, I'd like to have a rational conversation with you." I got up and went to pour him a glass of whisky, hoping it would help.

His lips curved into a small grin as he took a seat with a solid thump and took the glass from me. "Rational? As if I am anything but that." He took a sip, looking at me over the rim.

"Coy," Mom said. "Could you go see how long it'll be until dinner is ready? And let them know that your father is done with work."

She was just trying to get rid of me. "Mom, let me talk to my father."

"Yes, Fiona. Let him talk to me." Dad said as he held the drink with his two hands, and his jaw squared.

"I would like your permission to date Lila Stevens." I thought I should start there, just to see how bad his reaction would be.

"We've gone over this already, and I won't revisit the topic." He took another drink before asking my mother, "What's for dinner, anyway?"

"Chicken fried steak, mashed potatoes, cream gravy, and green beans." She smiled. "Coy's favorite and yours. You two have a lot in common. Don't you think so?"

"We have too much in common, that's the problem. Only I was brought up with a firm hand while our son was spared the rod." Putting down the glass, his haggard expression made him look like a man who'd made many mistakes in his life. "Spare the rod and spoil the child, as they say. And it seems that we've spoiled him."

"I am anything but spoiled. I grew up without my parents." I walked away, not wanting to say things that would hurt them, even if they didn't care that the things they said hurt me immensely. "You are all from a time that has to come to an end. You believe that money can separate the good from the bad—but you are wrong. You are wrong about so many things. And I hate that I'm just beginning to figure that out. I am from a family that I never really knew. And you did that to me, Dad. You sent me away so that I never got to chance to get to know any of you. Not really."

"Stay away from that girl, Coy," my father said. "Or you will hate the outcome."

"Maybe *you* will hate the outcome far worse than I will. Maybe *you* will find that losing your son—your only child— wasn't worth your fucking pride. This is a ranch—and one I barely even grew up on. A fucking ranch. Some goddamn dirt that cattle shit on all day long. It's not Camelot. It's not a kingdom. You are not royalty either. And I will do as I damn well please before I sacrifice my life for a piece of dirt that I hardly give two shits about!"

Leaving the room, I could feel the hot glare my father gave me. And I could hear my mother weeping.

But I didn't care.

LILA

Even though I had only seen Coy for a short time that night, I still fell asleep with a smile on my lips. I couldn't help but smile when I thought about our future together.

In only three days, we'd become man and wife. Coy had explained to me that I would need to pack as much as I could while being as discreet as possible.

After the marriage ceremony was to be performed by the local Justice of the Peace, Coy would take me to the used car lot to pick up the car that he'd bought me. And then we'd travel to Lubbock and move into the house his father had already bought him.

He was sure that his father would cut him off—at least for a while—but we'd stay at the house as long as we could. In the meantime, Coy would get a job to make ends meet. I was sure that I could find some way to make money to contribute to our household too.

Although terrified about everything, I was extremely excited to start a new life with the man I loved. I knew my family would cut me off for a while too. Not that there was much to cut me off from, other than communication. With time, they would come around. At least, I hoped.

My happy slumber was abruptly interrupted—I found myself

completely confused when I woke up with something pulling at me. My arms and legs were bound, and something was shoved into my mouth to keep me from making any noises that would alert the household to what was happening to me.

Dark shadows moved around me. One of these shadows snapped what sounded and resembled a paper bag. I then momentarily saw my oldest brother's face before the bag was put over my head.

With my hands tied at the wrists and my ankles bound together, I was helpless as one of them threw me over their shoulder and carried me out of my bedroom.

I felt the cool night air on my bare legs and arms, my slip of a nightgown offering no protection from the elements. I heard the sound of our car starting up, and then I was laid down on a hard surface. A whooshing sound was all I could hear before the slam of the trunk told me that I was being taken away from my home in the dead of night.

Tears started pouring down my face as I realized what this meant for my happy dreams. I knew something had to have happened to alert my father about the plans Coy and I had made. As worried as I was for myself, my heart held even more worry for Coy.

God, I hope they didn't do anything to him.

Even though I had no idea where they were taking me, I knew that my father and brothers were responsible—they were the ones who had done this to me. That knowledge alone made me feel slightly better as I knew that at least they wouldn't kill me.

Once I got to wherever they were taking me, I would figure out how to get back to Carthage and back to Coy. If I had to go directly to the police to make sure Coy was okay, then that's what I would do.

My father had no idea what he'd sparked inside of me. I was going to fight like a bear to return to the man I loved. If someone got hurt in the process, then too damn bad for them.

The car ride went on forever before we finally stopped. The trunk was opened, and I was picked up and tossed over someone's shoulder.

I heard what sounded like an old screen door opening with a loud squeak. "Bring her inside," I heard a woman say. "Back here. I've prepared a room for her."

Whoever this was, she'd been expecting me. I knew that meant this whole thing had been planned. And it had to have been planned recently since Coy and I had only gotten our marriage license the day before.

Someone had told on us. But I had no idea who even knew about our relationship. More worry for Coy built up inside of me and what might be happening to him at that moment.

I was dropped on what felt like a small bed, then something was wrapped around my waist, and I heard the click of a lock. "You've set this up very well, sister," I heard my father say, suspicion in his voice. "Who knew you had so much experience with restraints?"

"Never mind about that. You all leave. I'll deal with her now," the woman said.

"Are you sure that you can keep her here like this? For as long as it takes?" my father asked.

I had no idea what he was talking about. What was going to take so long? I wiggled and twisted on the bed, trying to free myself. Her voice came from somewhere right beside my head, "Don't do that, or I'll tighten the chains, Lila."

"Hilda," my father said, and I finally knew where I was. I was with my Aunt Hilda. "Make sure to take care of her—feed her well, and give her water too. I want my daughter back in a healthy state once this is over and done with."

"I won't kill her if that's what you're asking."

As soon as I heard the sound of their receding footsteps, leaving me alone, I let out a sigh of relief. At least I knew I was going to be okay. And as long as I had some strength left in me, I had a chance of escaping.

Knowing exactly where I was helped as well. My aunt had moved to Shreveport when I was just a baby. She hadn't come to Carthage ever since, but we'd gone to her house for several holidays during the past years. I remembered that it took about an hour to get there.

I'm only an hour away from home.

For the first time ever, I felt thankful that I'd never had a car. I was used to walking; I could walk several miles in a day without even getting tired. If I could make it to the highway, I was certain that I would be able to get a ride back to Carthage.

All I've got to do is free myself.

"Let's get that bag off your head," Hilda said as she came back into the room.

When she pulled the bag off my head, I blinked as the bare light bulb above the bed shined in my eyes. She pulled the gag out of my mouth and tossed it to the floor. "Thank you." I thought that if I was civil with her, she might see it fit to let me out of the chains sooner rather than later. "Aunt Hilda, why did they do this to me?"

"You've fallen for the wrong guy, honey. That's why you're here." She took a large pair of scissors and cut the zip ties that held my wrists and ankles together. "The chain around your waist will allow you to move around enough to get to that wastebasket over there. That will be your bathroom."

I looked at the small trashcan. "You want me to use the bathroom in that thing?" I couldn't keep the disgust and repulsion from my voice. "Why can't I use the bathroom?"

"Because the chain won't reach that far." She went to the door, then turned to look at me. "Take my advice, Lila. Put the Gentry boy out of your mind. He'll only cause you pain, sorrow, and loneliness. And you won't like that kind of life—believe me. I'll be back in a bit with some breakfast."

I wasn't hungry at all. All I wanted was to learn more about what had led me here. "Aunt Hilda, how do you know anything about the Gentry's? Did you know Coy's father?"

"No." She walked away, leaving me to my own thoughts.

I knew she had to have had something to do with someone in that family, and it must not have gone well. In fact, it must have gone horribly. There was no other reason for this insanity.

That meant she must have known Coy's father or grandfather because there wasn't anyone else. And the idea of her having an affair with the grandfather was pretty sickening.

As I lay there, trying to figure out what secret had led to all this, I started thinking about what I knew of Hilda. She had lived her whole life in Carthage, and then she had moved away all of a sudden.

I'd heard my mother and father talking about it on different occasions. They had both wondered why she had moved away when there was nothing for her in Shreveport.

Closing my eyes, I didn't really care what their damn secrets were. All I cared about was finding out if Coy was okay. "Aunt Hilda," I called out.

She came back to the door, leaning against the frame. "Yes."

"Is Coy okay? I have to know if he's okay."

She laughed as if that was the silliest question she'd ever heard. "He's a Gentry. Of course he's okay. *You've* been removed so that he can't get to you, but nothing has happened to him. I suppose his heart will ache when he finds that you've moved away without a word, but the boy is going to college soon anyway. He'll meet someone else, and he won't even spare you a thought. And that's when you can go back to your home with your father and mother. But not until then."

"So, I'm to be chained to this bed until that happens?" I'd never felt afraid of anyone in my family before, but everything that had happened in the last couple 0f hours was so far beyond normal that I didn't know how to feel anymore. I started to question how safe I was here—I was no longer certain that Aunt Hilda wouldn't harm me. This wasn't protection, this was punishment. It was more than punishment.

"I guess that depends on you, dear." She smiled as if she felt no empathy at all. "Whether or not you see the truth. This is a lesson on falling in love with a Gentry. Only pain comes with that. Once you've learned this lesson—however long it takes—then you, too, will have no desire to have him in your life anymore. And he'll have moved on long before."

Her words terrified me. Not because I believed them—Coy was a good man, he would never hurt me if he could help it—but because of the look in her eyes as she said them out loud. They were filled with nothing but bleakness. Whatever had happened to Aunt Hilda in the past, I knew it had made her believe in every word she was saying.

"I don't know which one of the Gentry's hurt you, Aunt Hilda, but I can assure you that Coy isn't like any of them. He's a good man. He's a caring man. He's not like his father or his grandfather." Suddenly, it occurred to me that she must be in contact with someone if she knew about Coy's plans for college. "Who are you talking to in the Gentry house?"

"That's none of your concern. You should be thinking about what you will do when you're taken back home. You'll want to get a job. You'll want to be able to take care of yourself."

That might have been the first bit of good advice she'd given me, and it made me wonder. "And where do you work, Aunt Hilda?"

"I don't." She turned and began walking away. "So, you won't be alone here in the house, if you were thinking you could escape. I'll be right here at all times. Even my groceries will be brought to me to make sure you don't have a moment all by yourself."

"So, someone is paying you to keep me here." I knew my family had no money for that. But the Gentry's had more than enough.

❦ 18 ❦

COY

As usual, I went to the park in town where Lila and I would meet each morning at six—so we could watch the sunrise together. Only she wasn't there. I went back just after dark, too, for our usual second meeting of the day. Again, she wasn't there. I waited for her until midnight, but she still never showed up.

The next day was the same. That's when I really started to worry. The day after was supposed to be our wedding day. I knew I had to do something to find out where she was and what the hell was going on.

Has she changed her mind about marrying me?

If the marriage was something she'd grown concerned about, we didn't have to go through with it. I loved her and wanted to marry her, but I didn't want to force her or make her feel pressured into doing something she didn't want.

I needed to talk to her to let her know my thoughts. I needed to see her, touch her, kiss her. It had only been a couple of days, but I missed her more than I knew I could miss anyone.

Since I knew where she lived, on the morning we were supposed to get married, I parked on the street from her family's small house. Waiting for someone to emerge from the house, I finally saw two young teens walking out, heading towards the opposite direction of my truck.

Following them at a distance, I drove slowly so they wouldn't notice me. One of the boys split from the other, went up to a house, and headed inside as the other kept walking.

Taking my chance, I pulled up next to the boy and rolled my window down. "Hi. You're Lila's little brother, right?"

"Yeah." He looked at my truck. "You're the guy she doesn't want to see anymore, aren't you?"

I shook my head. "Is your sister home?"

"My sister moved away a couple of nights ago. Dad told us that she wanted to get away from this town." A frown told me he missed his sister. "Cause of some guy."

"She didn't tell you goodbye?"

"No. Dad said that she woke him up, and she was crying. She said she wanted to leave because she couldn't face this guy she's been seeing, but she didn't want to see him anymore. So Dad took her to live with our aunt. He told us that when her heart is better, she'll be back. But that might take a long time."

There was no way in hell I would believe that story. But this kid seemed to believe all of it. "You miss her, don't you?"

"Yeah. Lila's a great sister. She always hangs out with me and my brother, even when nobody else gives us the time of day. And she cooks for us, too. She makes the best grilled cheese sandwiches in the world." He wiped his eyes with the palms of his hands. "I didn't think she was sad. I'd never seen her happier. But I'm just a kid, so what do I know about things like that anyway?"

I bet he knew a lot more than he realized.

I had to get the address of where she'd gone. But I highly doubted the boy knew it. "I'd love to write her. We were just friends." I didn't want him thinking I was the guy she'd run away from. "But I'd like to keep in touch with her. You know, let her know that she's missed around here."

"Oh." He looked at the ground, scuffing his bare feet across it to kick up dust.

He wasn't catching on at all. "So, do you think that you can find out the address for me? I could meet you at the park at the end of the street just before dark tonight so that you can give it to me. I've got a few bucks I can give you if you do that for me."

His dark eyes lit up. "You'll pay me to get you the address?"

"Sure." I needed him to keep it a secret, though. "I'll give you a whole twenty bucks if you can get it without letting anyone know what you're doing." I reached into my pocket and pulled out a ten, then held it out to him. "Here, take this as a sign of good faith. And I'll give you that twenty when you come to the park with the address. Make sure to write it down, so you don't forget any of it."

The way he stared at the money in his hand told me he wasn't used to seeing it there. "Wow!"

"I know, right? Wait until you're holding twice that amount in your hand. Do we have a deal? And what's your name, by the way."

"Paul." He looked at me. "And your name is?"

"John," I lied. "I'll see you at the park just before dark. If we have a deal."

"We've got a deal! I'll be there. I do know this much, she's staying with my father's sister—Aunt Hilda. She lives in Shreveport, Louisiana."

Only about an hour away!

"Cool. Well, see if you can get me that address so I can send her a letter. I'll make sure to tell her how you helped me out, Paul. Anything you'd like me to tell her from you?"

"Tell her that I love her and that I miss her and her grilled cheese sandwiches. And I hope her heart gets better very quickly so she can come back home."

"I'll do that. See you later, Paul." I drove away, feeling slightly better about things.

One thing I was pretty sure of was that someone had told her father about us. And I was sure he'd taken Lila to his sister's against her will.

As I drove back home, I had to wonder if my father or even my mother had had anything to do with Lila's father finding out about us. I'd just had that talk with my parents the night before Lila stopped showing up—the night her little brother said she'd asked her father to take her away.

Could my parents really be this heartless?

Once I got home, I walked into the house and went straight up to my bedroom, not wanting to talk to anyone. Ditching my boots at the door, I walked inside and fell face down on my bed.

Nothing made sense to me. I felt as if I didn't know my own family. Sure, I'd grown up in boarding school, but I did spend summers with them, and all the holidays too. For the first year, I'd even been picked up to come home for the weekends. But in all that time—or that little time—I had missed out on learning who my family really was.

My mother and father had always been strong figures to me. But now I could see that my father ran roughshod over my mother. My mother's strong façade was just that—fake.

Then there was my father. He said the right words to me, telling me he did everything for my own good. But those words were spoken merely to pay me lip service.

When it came down to it, everything he did was for his own best interest and no one else's. Who I dated should have never been any of their concern. And now it seemed that my own family might go so far as to take away the person who meant the most to me in my life.

What was worse was that they might have pushed Lila away from all the people she knew and loved. She had friends and family in Carthage. I just knew that somehow, someone in my own family must've made sure her father got her out of town, away from me.

Whatever had happened to forge a line of steel between our families didn't have a damn thing to do with either of us. We shouldn't have been put in the middle of their stupid feud. We should've been left alone.

Rolling over, I saw the clock on my nightstand.

Noon. We should've already been married by this time today.

Getting up, I went to my dresser. I'd made a fake bottom in the middle drawer to hide the things I couldn't let my parents find. The thousands of dollars in cash, the marriage license, and the wedding rings I'd bought two days earlier.

I'd been so excited to show them to Lila. But I'd never gotten the chance.

This was unjust, unfair, and unacceptable. I had to put a stop to this. I couldn't let my family continue acting this way.

And more than anything, I needed to make sure that Lila was okay.

I heard the sound of a telephone ringing in the distance and knew it was coming from my parent's bedroom down the hall. At the time, with my mother's injuries and her being in a wheelchair, my father was the only one using that room.

When I heard the ringing stop, I got up and crept along the wall, being careful not to make a sound. Placing my ear against the door, I could hear my father talking. "This isn't an open invitation to keep in contact with me."

Who would he say something like that to?

"He's here. Yes, I'm sure. I saw his truck in the driveway. How would he ever find your place?"

The hair on the back of my neck stood up. I was sure that he was talking to whoever had Lila. And Paul had said she was with her Aunt Hilda.

"So what if she said that? He has no idea who you are or where you are. Plus, I'm going to suggest that he and I take a trip to Lubbock to check out his new house. I think that'll help take his mind off of her."

I knew it!

"What do you mean, you have a gun?" my father asked with concern. "If he somehow finds her, you better not harm a hair on his head. Do you hear me? Do you?"

I did not like the sound of that. Not only because it put me in danger, but it meant that this person who was keeping Lila from me—Hilda—wasn't afraid to use violence. And that bothered me to no end. If I weren't there, who would protect Lila?

"Just don't open the door if he somehow finds you. Don't let him in. Act as if no one is home, for God's sake. Do I have to give you explicit instructions on every little thing? Damn."

Even though I was hearing the words come out of my father's mouth, it was still unbelievably hard to imagine that he could do such a horrible thing—not only to his only child but to Lila, too.

He made someone leave their home just to keep them away from me.

I had no idea what I should do. I loved Lila with my whole heart and soul. I would do anything for her. I would even lay down my life for her.

She didn't deserve to be treated this way. She didn't deserve to be taken from her own home, and away from the town she grew up in. She didn't deserve any of this.

I'd already felt terrible that my family wouldn't accept her. And now they'd gone and turned her entire life upside down.

I felt as if I was some sort of poison to her. All I wanted to do was love her. But the people I came from had not only forbidden it, but they had done whatever they could to put it to a stop.

My father surely had no heart. Any parent who did something this heinous to their child was pure evil.

All Lila and I wanted was to love each other the same way everyone else got to. We weren't asking for much—and yet, look at what had happened.

For the first time, I wondered if maybe Lila was better off if I stayed out of her life.

❧ 19 ❧

LILA

Wearing a white cotton dress, I walked down an empty aisle to meet Coy, who stood at the front of the room. He wore a suit and a tie and looked more handsome than I'd ever seen him.

My heart raced as I walked up to him and took his hand into mine. "Coy Gentry, I take you to be my lawfully wedded husband."

"And I take you, Lila Stevens, to be my lawfully wedded wife."

We kissed, and the next thing I knew, we were in bed, rolling around naked and laughing as we made love. Sunlight shone through the window as birds chirped and sang outside.

Life would be better now that we were joined as one. Things would change. Coy and I would live life on our own terms.

"I love you, Lila Gentry." Coy looked down at me as he moved his body over mine.

He pressed himself into me, making me sigh. "I love you too, my handsome husband."

Moving like waves on the ocean, we made love, holding each other, laughing, sighing, and even crying over the beauty of it all. We were husband and wife—and no one could come between us anymore. No one could separate what God had joined together.

"Wake up," I heard someone calling.

Startled, I woke up with my eyes swimming in tears. Wiping them away, disappointment resonated within me as I realized it had only been a dream.

Coy and I were supposed to get married that very day. But I was still chained up, unable to get to the courthouse where we'd agreed to meet at eight in the morning.

Hilda put the plate of food on the bedside table. "Here."

"What time is it?" I asked as I sat up.

"Does it really matter?" She walked towards the small television she'd brought in for me. Turning it on, she stood there in front of it for a moment. "Days go by. Time goes by. And nothing—absolutely nothing—changes." She turned to face me. "That's life when you love a Gentry man."

"When are you going to tell me what went on between you and Mr. Gentry?" I still wasn't sure which one of them she'd been with, but I was certain that she'd been with one of them.

"Eat your eggs before they get cold." She walked out of the room, then came back with a bucket of water, a washcloth, and some clean clothes for me to put on. "After you eat, wash yourself and then put these on. You reek."

"It *has* been three days." I wouldn't be ashamed of stinking when I'd been kept away from the bathroom and clean clothes.

She went to the trash can that served as my toilet. She picked it up and held it away from her as she left the room. Again, I felt no shame in having used the only thing she gave me—it was her shame, not mine.

I smiled as a thought crossed my mind—what if I could make the room stink so badly that she would have to set me free? Even if only to make me clean it myself. And then I would hit her in the head with whatever I could find and run away.

I looked at the panties she'd given me. They were huge and an ugly tan color. And the other piece of clothing was just an old, threadbare nightgown in a greyish color.

I supposed she thought I wouldn't dare run outside in such a sad outfit. But she was wrong. If I had no clothes on, I was still going to make a run for it as soon as I got the chance. I'd use tree branches to cover my body if I had to.

When she came back in with the cleaned trashcan with a new liner inside, she placed it right back where she'd picked it up from. "You still haven't finished eating yet?"

"No." I saw no reason to hurry. I'd been civil, and that had gotten me nowhere, but I still tried. "I don't think you're getting paid enough to deal with this. Do you?"

She laughed. "I have to agree with you. But I'm not in charge."

"Then who is?"

"Someone." She left me alone again.

I took my time eating. Then I pulled off the clothes I'd been wearing the night I was abducted from my own bed. Tossing them into the trashcan, I saw no reason to keep them. They were soiled and ripped from the rough treatment I'd had to undergo.

Washing my body with the cold water, I tried not to cry. I had to be strong. I couldn't let myself get run down or worn out. The idea here was to break my spirit and my love for Coy. It wasn't going to work, though.

I knew he'd wait for me. I knew he wouldn't find someone else to love, not with things unresolved between us. No matter what he'd been told, I knew his heart belonged to me, and mine belonged to him. I had to believe he was telling himself the same thing.

His parents didn't understand him. He was a passionate, independent man who stood up for what he believed in. He was the way he was because of what they had done to him when he was a little kid. Sending him away at only six years to live with strangers—it had turned him into a different sort of young man.

He'd never really felt loved, he'd told me once. And now that he had felt my love, he wouldn't let it go. I prayed he knew that I wasn't about to let it go either.

They could only keep us apart for so long. My friends would be stopping by the house to ask for me. Janine would keep bothering my family until they told her where I was. Or she might even go to her parents to seek help to find me.

I also had high hopes that Coy wouldn't believe whatever garbage he was told about my disappearance. I hoped he would know that my father had taken me somewhere and that he'd maybe even go to the cops.

Someone had to do something. Someone had to miss me and want to know where I was. I had good friends. I knew that they could get together and demand to know my whereabouts.

But will they?

All of my friends knew that my father could be a real asshole. And he had control over my older brothers, making them real assholes too. So, there was a chance that they wouldn't want to deal with them, and they might not try that hard to get information about me.

My mind infuriated me. I would be thinking positively for one minute, and then it would flip on me and take me down a desolate road—a road with no help along it.

Getting dressed with a chain around one's waist was a real pain in the ass, and when I caught Hilda snickering at me as she walked back into the room, I clenched my jaw. "You know, a real shower would be nice."

"I bet it would. Just think how much better it's going to feel when you haven't had one in months." She looked around the room. "Where are your dirty clothes?"

"I threw them away." I shimmied the gown down my body after shoving it through the chain, which only gave about a half-inch gap around my body.

She went and retrieved them from the trash. "I'll wash them. You'll wear them again."

I wasn't about to waste my breath arguing with her. It didn't matter what the hell I wore anyway. "Why are you doing this to me, Hilda?"

She stopped and looked at me. "Why should you get something when I couldn't have it?" And then she left.

I sat down on the bed, wondering what, exactly, that meant. *Did she want to marry Coy's dad or grandfather?*

Since no one had told me why I'd been taken away, I had no idea what they exactly knew about me and Coy. Maybe no one knew about the marriage we'd been planning. Maybe they just found out that we'd been seeing each other in secret.

So, did she mean that she had wanted a secret relationship with one of the Gentry men and hadn't gotten it?

As I fell back onto the bed, I rested my hand on my forehead. My brain hurt from all the thinking I'd been doing.

I knew this much. It did not matter what Hilda or any of the Gentry's had done in the past. What mattered was me and Coy. What mattered was my life. And that meant I had to figure out how I was going to get out of the damn chain and out of the damn house.

Feeling frustrated, I said to myself out loud, "Coy will figure out where I am, and he will come for me."

Eventually, I did figure out what time it was. When the daytime soap opera that my mother watched came on the little television, I knew it was noon.

And not long after the show started, I heard Hilda talking on the phone to someone. "Hey, it's me." There was a pause before she added, "Is he there with you right now? Are you sure? I don't know. I mean, she said something about him coming to get her. It's got me worried."

She's got to be talking to someone in Coy's family.

"I've got a gun. I'll use it if I have to," she said, building up fear inside of me. I sat up, trying to hear each and every word she spoke.

Would she really shoot Coy if he came for me? Would she shoot me if I tried to leave?

I never would have thought it of anyone in my family, but she had me chained up to a bed, using a trash can as a toilet. I could no longer predict what she would or wouldn't do.

"I hear you. But what am I to do if he shows up here?"

Does she really have any reason to believe that Coy might be able to find me?

"I'm sorry that I called you. I'll deal with things on my own—as usual." I heard her slamming down the phone, cursing under her breath. "Damn that selfish man. Damn him to hell for all he's done and put me through. When will this torture end?"

Now I knew for certain that there was something between my aunt and one of Coy's relatives. My gut was telling me it was his father who Hilda had a past with.

If Coy's father was against our relationship, then it made sense that his father before him must've felt the same way if he'd been seeing my aunt. She was from the poor side of town, too, just like me.

The two of them must've been forbidden from being together. But had they really stayed away from each other, or had they had a secret relationship the same way Coy and I had?

And why do I keep caring about that?

That didn't amount to a hill of beans. Who cared about their past?

Knowing the truth wouldn't help me get out of the situation I was in. Coy and I weren't going to follow the archaic rules of the Gentry family. We were going to get married and live our own lives—far away from Carthage, if our marriage wasn't accepted by our families.

We had love. We had tons of it. And when you have the kind of love, you don't need anything or anyone else. You could live on that alone.

Somehow, I had to get free. Coy and I had to show our

families that they couldn't stop love. Not a love as true and faithful as ours.

I closed my eyes and pictured Coy's face as I repeated silently, *I am in Shreveport with my Aunt Hilda. Come find me. Go through your father's things to find the address if you have to. I have no doubt that he has it.*

The phone call I'd overheard also confirmed my suspicions that Coy's father was paying my aunt to keep me away. I bet he'd paid for a lot of things—things that his wife didn't know a damn about.

Keep fucking with me, and I might well end your marriage, Mr. Gentry!

20

COY

Anger coursed through my veins as I stood outside my father's door. I made a quick knock before opening it and barging in. "And to whom are you telling my whereabouts?"

He stood by the desk in his bedroom, looking at me with wide eyes—eyes that held a fair amount of fear in them. "I wasn't telling anyone anything about you, Coy."

I had a sharp memory, so he wasn't going to get away with that. "I heard you say these exact words: *'He's here. Yes, I'm sure. I saw his truck in the driveway. How would he ever find your place?'"*

"*He* could be anybody, Coy. What makes you think I was talking about you?" His mouth was working hard to convince me that I was wrong. But it was his dark eyes, wide open, that told me I was right on point.

"Okay, then tell me who *she* is. I heard everything you just said on that call. About me not knowing who the person on the phone was, about your idea of a little trip to Lubbock to take my mind off of *her*. Who else has a new house in Lubbock besides me? And who else needs his attention taken off a girl? Don't try to lie to me, Dad. I've found you out."

"You're not being reasonable. You're acting like a frenzied

animal, son. You need to calm down, and I'll explain the conversation you eavesdropped on—a conversation meant to be private."

"Oh, I'm sure you wanted that conversation to remain private, Dad. Especially the part about a gun."

My father turned away from me so I could no longer witness the shocked and rather pitiful expression on his face. "You didn't hear that right, son. I never said anything about a gun. I don't know why you think you can remember so much of what was said, but you didn't get it right. Sorry that you've misunderstood everything, but I was talking about one of the ranch hands who's been having some family troubles. I'm not at liberty to talk about his private affairs with you either, or I would fill you in on the whole sordid story."

"Dad, I was in every one of the school plays while I was in boarding school, not that you came to any of them. I've got a great memory for words, so I know I recall everything perfectly and exactly as you meant it."

He walked away from me, ignoring what I'd said, and grabbed his car keys off the dresser. "I've got tons to do today, Coy, otherwise, I'd love to stay here and play this little game of nonsense with you."

"Tell me what the name Hilda means to you, Dad." I inhaled, preparing myself for his reaction.

He laughed as if that was some sort of joke. "I went to school with Hilda Stevens, if that's who you're talking about. She's that girl's aunt. Don't know why you're asking me about her, though."

"I have reason to believe that you know a lot more about that woman than you're letting on." I crossed my arms over my chest and stood in the doorway so he couldn't leave. "I'd like to know more about her."

"Why? Because she's the girl's aunt?" he asked as he took a seat on the bed, crossing his arms over his chest to mimic my posture.

"Sure, let's say that's the reason why." He knew that I had some suspicions now, and I could tell it made him uneasy. I watched as his eyes started darting around the room instead of staying on mine.

"Well, she was shy and quiet in school. I never heard her say much of anything. She moved out of town a while back. Not that I know why. I just heard it through the grapevine. I don't know much about most people around this town—Hilda Stevens included.

"Stevens?" I asked, finding that a little odd. Paul had told me that Hilda was his father's sister, but he hadn't told me she still went by her maiden name. "She's your age and still has her maiden name?"

"As far as I know, she never married. So what?" he asked as if it wasn't a big deal.

"So what? Why didn't she ever get married? She never had a boyfriend?" My suspicions about my father's past involvement with the Stevens were coming to fruition.

"I don't know, son. I wasn't close to the girl. I got married fresh out of college, if you will recall. I didn't care about what anyone else in this town was doing. I've got to get going." He got off the bed and walked toward me. "You can come and give me a hand if you want. There's a cow in labor in the barn, and the vet might need all the help he can get."

The last thing I wanted to do was help my father or grandfather on the ranch. Not when it was the very thing that made them think they were better than other people. "No thanks."

I walked back to my bedroom. Knowing he would be busy in the barn, I decided I would take that time to pack some things and get ready for whatever was coming. I didn't exactly know what that would be, but I had to do something.

I was supposed to meet up with Lila's little brother a little before dark, and I'd have the address then. I could get on my way to Lila, and once I had her, I wouldn't be bringing her back anywhere near here. I wasn't about to take her any place where she wouldn't be safe—not until I had changed her last name to mine.

I'd snuck out one day with the keys to the house in Lubbock that my father kept in the desk drawer in his bedroom. I'd had a couple of copies made for me and Lila, and had hidden them in the drawer with our other things.

It was time to take my stash out so as to have it with me at all times. I wasn't sure how things were going to play out, so I wanted to be ready for whatever was coming.

One thing I knew for sure was that I wouldn't be backing down to anyone when I returned home with Lila. And neither would she.

If Lila was still up for marrying me, I wouldn't bring her back to Carthage until we were legally married. If my parents refused to accept our marriage, then that would be their loss.

In the late evening, after I'd managed to get everything to my truck, I walked through the living room to see if my mother was there.

She looked up at me as I came into the room. "You look nice. Where are you off to tonight?"

"Some guys are having a party. There's going to be drinking too. I'm gonna crash at one of my friend's houses so that I don't have to drive. Gotta be responsible."

Nodding, she asked, "What's the friend's name? I did teach most of the people in your age group, you know."

I hadn't thought of that. "Oh, his name is Paul. He's not from here. I think that's why we get along so well. He's sort of an outsider—like me."

"I hope you don't really feel like an outsider here, Coy. You belong in this town, just like everybody else. You're going to be a huge part of the community someday when you take over this ranch. You know, it's a big employer." She looked around quickly as if to see if anyone would overhear her next words. "You can do things differently than your father and grandfather once you take over."

I looked around the big living room. I'd never thought of this place as my home. I'd grown up and spent the majority of my time at the boarding school. In my mind, I hadn't ever had a real home or a real family. I'd certainly never thought of this place as mine.

I also knew next to nothing about ranching. All I could do was ride a horse and listen to my father order the ranch hands around. I supposed he thought he was teaching me to do what he did. But since he never explained himself—ever— in reality, I wasn't being taught a damn thing.

Nevertheless, her words struck me. I could do things differently than my father. She didn't know it, but that was exactly what I was doing. I wasn't about to let history repeat itself —not that I exactly knew what that history was.

"Yeah, I know. Maybe I'll learn more in college. I just don't have the experience Dad has with the ranch. I'm not sure I'm cut out to run it."

"You'll learn. Once you get done with college, you'll come home, and you'll learn how to run the place. It's your legacy, Coy. You were born to take over this ranch."

I didn't want it. I didn't want to have anything to do with it. Now that I was pretty sure my father had interfered with my relationship with Lila as much as he had, I didn't want anything to do with him or my grandparents.

Mom was the one person I wasn't sure I wanted to cut out of my life. But I wasn't even completely sure about her.

"Yeah, we'll see what college does for me."

"You don't want to stay for dinner and eat before you go to this party? We're having steak and baked potatoes tonight." She smiled at me, and it made my heart hurt.

Both of my parents kept trying to act like all the arguments and the accusations I'd made during the last few days hadn't happened at all. I didn't want to feel this way. I wanted things to be the way they had always been. I wanted back the family that I'd thought I had. I wanted that to be real. And it seemed that they wanted that too.

So much dishonesty. So many secrets. But the manipulation, the bullying, and the horrible deeds were too much to take. I didn't even want to eat a meal with my family at that time.

It was all I could do to pretend that nothing was wrong. But I knew I had to do that if I didn't want them to stop me—or try to, anyway—from leaving the house.

No matter what my father had said, he knew that I was right about what I had overheard. And that meant he'd be thinking that I might go renegade on him.

It had never been my intention to ruin my parents' marriage. But if they wanted to ruin my relationship with the woman I loved, then a turn about was fair play.

If I found Lila with her Aunt Hilda, and I got Hilda to confess about having a relationship with my father, either prior to his marriage to my mother or afterward, then I was going to use that information to my advantage.

"There's gonna be food there, Mom. See you tomorrow. I'll most likely sleep in, so don't expect me to be here early or anything. You probably won't see me before afternoon." I went over and kissed her on the cheek, feeling as if I might just cry.

I loved my mother. Out of everyone in that house, she had a good heart. It was just that my father knew how to control her. How to use that good heart and hold it over her head.

"I love you, Coy." She hugged me tightly. "So much."

"Me too, Mom." I hugged her back, then pulled away and turned around so that she wouldn't see my tear-glossed eyes.

Damn, I hate that it's come to this.

21

LILA

Listening to my aunt mutter to herself for an hour after the phone call, I got the distinct impression that things between her and Coy's father had been much more serious than I'd assumed.

Initially, I thought they might have had an ill-fated young fling. Now, I was starting to suspect there might have been an affair. Or maybe the two of them had been secret lovers before he got married, and then he went off to college and came back with a wife. But she mumbled some things that made it seem as if they'd had a very long and extremely intimate relationship. One that had ended before she was ready for it to be over.

I heard a pot slam down on the stove, and then she muttered, "I gave him everything I had." Something else crashed, and I thought she must've thrown it. "Children. All for him!"

I sat there, mesmerized by what she was saying. *She gave up children for him? How?*

"How can he still hurt me this way?" she mumbled as something else crashed to the floor. "Why do I allow it?"

On and on she went. And I sat there, listening to every word.

Then she came into my room with dinner. "I burnt the meatloaf. The potatoes are lumpy. The tomato gravy has too much salt." She put down the plate on the bedside table, then turned to leave.

"Aunt Hilda, would you like to bring your plate in here and eat with me?" I wanted to know more. I wanted her to feel comfortable with me so she would confide in me.

It was purely manipulative, and I knew that. But I needed some ammunition if I was going to be able to get out of this prison.

"I'm not going to be good company. And I don't know why you would want to eat with me in the first place. I am your jailer, after all." She left me before I could think of anything to say.

But she came back with a glass of water, so I got another chance to gain her trust. "You know that I could hear how angry you were with whoever you were talking to earlier. I do have ears. And I do have compassion for a woman who has been hurt. Why don't you come sit with me, and tell me why you're so upset?"

She leaned against the doorframe, her head cocked to one side, and her hands clasped in front of her. "Lila, my only dear niece, you would never, not even in a million years, understand why I am such a bitter old woman."

"Try me." I took a bite of the meatloaf. It was burnt, but I acted as if I liked it anyway. "Hey, this isn't bad at all. I like it."

"I was a shy girl when I was younger." She left the room after that, and I wondered what had happened. But then she returned with a glass of red wine. She leaned back against the doorframe as she took a sip. "When I look back on it now, I realize that I was an easy target."

"Who targeted you?" I took a bite of the lumpy potatoes. "These are good too."

"You're only saying that because your mother is a horrible cook." She sighed. "Your mother was able to get a good man. But not me."

"Well, my father isn't that good." He was mean and strict.

Plus, he'd kidnapped his own daughter, so he had an evil streak as well.

"I mean that he did the right thing by your mother—even though she couldn't cook worth a damn. And let's face it, she's got the brain of a turnip."

My mother wasn't completely stupid. But I wanted to pull Hilda in, so I agreed. "Yes, she's so ignorant."

"Yet, as ignorant as she is, she got a husband. She got to have children with this man. She's someone's wife. Even if she doesn't deserve it." She took another drink, then held the glass with both hands. "I can cook like a chef. I can clean better than the finest maid. And I can please a man better than any woman I know."

My cheeks heated with her words. I had the idea that my aunt had been quite a woman—despite what years of what I now saw as bitterness had done to her, she was still an attractive woman. I could only imagine what she must've looked like when she was young and full of hope. And yet, no man had ever taken the time to get to know her.

"You know, maybe it's your quiet demeanor that's kept you single all this time. One of my mother's older sisters lost her husband last year to cancer. She's going to church on the lookout for men she might be attracted to."

"Church isn't a place I would find the right kind of man. Anyway, my heart no longer belongs to me. I don't have it to give to any other man."

"And why can't you be with the man who has your heart?" I was sure that was because he was already married.

"It doesn't matter. It never has." She downed the glass, finishing it off, then leaving me once more.

I took another bite as I waited to see if she'd come back. Although she'd said that she could cook like a chef and clean a house like the finest maid, I found the food bad, and the cleanliness of my room and what I could see outside it to be wanting.

She's delusional—and depressed.

Who wouldn't be if they were in her place?

I heard the sound of her sweeping up the things she'd probably thrown on the floor. Then I heard her gathering them into a dustpan before throwing them into the trash.

She went from one thing to another, cleaning up the house. And then she came into my room. "You're done with your food, right?"

I'd eaten every bite, even though it wasn't that good. "Yes, Aunt Hilda. Thank you."

She smiled at me. "You're going to make a fine woman someday, Lila. You don't let things hold you back."

SHE CARRIED MY EMPTY PLATE OUT OF THE ROOM, AND WHEN SHE came back, she had brought a broom with her and began sweeping. "I've got to get this place clean. I've been letting things go, and that's not like me at all."

"Are you depressed?" I asked as I watched her move with grace while doing such a mundane chore.

"Yes," she said so quickly that it made no sense. Not many people were willing to share something like that—at least not so quickly.

"Is it because you're in this place all alone?"

She nodded. "Yes."

"Then why don't you move back to Carthage, where your family is? You would have plenty of company if you moved back there."

She didn't say a word as she finished sweeping and then left the room again, only to return with a dustpan. She bent over to collect the dirt she'd gathered in a pile. "If I could, I would." With that, she left again.

I sat there wondering why in the hell she couldn't move back if she wanted to. As soon as she returned again with a mop bucket in one hand and a mop in the other, I asked, "Is it because you don't have enough money or a job?"

"No." She plunged the mop into the bucket, then began from the far end of the small room, mopping with such precision and grace that stupefied me.

"You love sweeping and mopping, don't you?" I asked as I watched her almost dance with the mop.

"I do." She laughed. "I used to love doing housework. I loved to make it fun and exciting." She shrugged her shoulders. "And pleasurable."

I'd never heard of anyone calling housework pleasurable. "Do you mind telling me how you make yourself see chores as pleasurable?"

She stopped mopping and leaned against the handle. "Well, you're chained up, aren't you?"

"I am." I had no idea what she was getting at.

"And if you were let out of those chains after the three days, you would find pleasure in being able to move around, wouldn't you?"

"I suppose I would." I still had no idea what she was driving at.

"So, if you were set free and told to clean the house, then you would find some freedom in being able to move around. And that alone would give you pleasure. Such a simple thing can give one so much pleasure." She closed her eyes, and a smile curved her lips. "And if you had the right kind of man, he would treat you to something nice after a job well done."

"Something nice?" I wasn't following her at all. My father didn't give my mother anything for cleaning the house. He'd never even made a comment about it—he just expected her to do it.

"You know, a trinket of some kind. And that would be followed by a nice long bath together, where he'd wash your body and hair. And then you would do the same for him. You would take care of each other—in all ways."

"A trinket for cleaning a house? I'd rather get a gift because a man loved and respected me, not because I performed some duty well for him." Her idea seemed a little transactional—a little old-fashioned. Not only that, but a bit demeaning as well. I liked the idea of being equals. "And you said something about being chained up and then set free? That sounds pretty bad to me, especially if you're only being let free to clean the house." This was maybe one of the weirdest conversations I'd ever had.

"It's not bad at all." She began mopping again. "When a man really takes care of you, it's the best feeling in the world. You don't have to make any decisions because he makes them for you. And he takes care of everything for you too. There are absolutely no worries."

Except being chained up, apparently.

I had no idea what my aunt was into. But her moving away from her family was finally making sense to me. And the connection between her and the Gentry's was becoming even more worrisome.

Mrs. Gentry was a good woman. If her husband was some sort of abuser, she didn't deserve it.

I thought about seeing her in the wheelchair at Coy's party. I had to wonder if there really was an accident or if her husband had been the one to put her in those leg casts.

Is Mr. Gentry into hurting women for his own pleasure?

Though I was young, I wasn't naïve. I had older brothers, and gossip about people's lives—even the most intimate parts—was rampant in our neighborhood.

I had to find out more. "So, this being chained up, and then set free to do housework and take a bath together…does it also involve something a little more—let's say—taboo?"

"Spanking can come into play if the sub has earned it. Or she might just want it. Subs can find themselves needing discipline for things that happened a long time ago, things that they might've gotten away with."

Drunk Aunt Hilda was much more informative than sober Aunt Hilda. I tried to keep my blush under control. I'd heard my brothers whisper that word before—sub—when Mrs. Richards down the street had been caught having an affair. I needed to hear her admit more, though. "You should tell me all about this stuff. I had no idea this was a thing."

"It's been a thing for years. Centuries even." Her eyes turned glassy as she looked up. "I miss being a sub to my master. I miss it more than I miss anything else."

Holy shit! What has my aunt been into—and with whom?

22

COY

I sat in my truck, waiting for Paul to show up at the park near his house. Twilight came and went, leaving me in the darkness. But still, I waited, hoping like hell that he'd come through for me.

He may have had trouble getting the address. Or he might've had trouble getting out of the house for some reason. And now that it was dark, he might've been unable to leave the house.

I had no idea what kept him away. But I knew I had to stay right where I had told him I would be, or I might miss my chance to find Lila.

An hour after the sun had set, I saw a shadow moving up the road. I watched as it got closer and closer, seemingly coming towards my truck.

My heart pounded hard in my chest as I started feeling hopeful that I would soon be able to find Lila. Only three days had passed, but to me, they felt like years.

"John?"

Breathing a sigh of relief, I answered, "Yeah, it's me, Paul. Did you get me the address?"

He came up to the side of the truck. "Yeah. My mom keeps everyone's addresses and phone numbers in a book by the phone in the kitchen. It was easy to get the address. I don't want you to pay me anything else since it wasn't hard to get."

I handed him a twenty-dollar bill anyway. "A deal is a deal, Paul." As I gave him the money, he gave me the slip of paper that held my world on it. 'Thanks, man."

He shuffled back and forth a little as if he was nervous. "You promise not to tell that guy she was seeing about this, right?"

"I promise." The way he acted made me a little uneasy. "Did your father tell you something more about her leaving? Is that why you're late? Were you thinking about not giving me the address?"

"Sort of," he confessed. "I heard my mom and dad talking this afternoon. Mom was asking about Lila. She's feeling bad that Lila hadn't come to her to talk to her about her boy problems."

Because she didn't have any.

"Oh, so she didn't say anything to your mom about why she wanted to leave town?" I found that odd. Mostly because after her father had forbidden her to see me, she'd told me that he was an ass. It made no sense that he was the one she had gone to if she needed help getting out of town.

"Not a word. So, Mom's been asking Dad every day if he's heard from Lila. Each day he says that he has and that Lila just wants to be left alone." He shrugged. "Girls, I can't figure them out."

If Lila had truly wanted to get away from me, I knew she would want to talk to her mother about things, not to her father. She definitely wouldn't be calling to give him updates—she would be calling her mother. "So, why hasn't your mother just given Lila a call herself?"

"She has called our Aunt Hilda, who Lila's staying with. Aunt Hilda has told her every time that Lila is resting and she doesn't want to wake her, but that she's doing fine. She even said that Lila's told her that she might want to remain with her and get a job up there in Shreveport."

That does sound a little bit more legit than anything her father has said. "Why do you think she really left, Paul?"

"I overheard my father yelling at her at the beginning of summer. He told her that she couldn't see this guy named Gentry —that's his last name, I think. And she was mad at our dad for telling her that." He laughed as he shook his head. "But she must've been seeing this guy anyway—even without our father's consent. Dad said that she told him that she couldn't keep seeing that guy because if she did, he was going to be disowned by his family, and he would lose everything. She said that she couldn't be the one responsible for him losing his inheritance, which is tons of money and a huge ranch. I think that's why she left—not because he was a bad guy or anything."

Crap. That makes sense.

But what about the call I heard at home? Could my dad have been telling me the truth? My trust in my family had been shaken the past few months, but maybe I was hearing things that weren't real.

"Do you think she'll stay up there and get a job?" I was on the fence about going to get her now that I heard all this.

With a shrug, he said, "Who knows? I just know that I'm gonna miss her if she stays up there. Anyway, I've gotta go. I'm supposed to be outside feeding the dog. Someone might notice that I haven't come back into the house yet."

"Thanks, Paul."

"Yeah, thanks for the money, John." He ran off into the night, and I had an inkling that I would most probably never see the kid again.

Looking at the address, I continued second-guessing myself, wondering what I should do. Maybe Lila had left because she wanted to. Maybe I should just go ahead and move to Lubbock so that she returns back home. I could write her a letter, telling her that I knew she'd left so I wouldn't lose everything. I could write that I left Carthage and that she could come back home to her family and friends.

It's not like I had anyone except her in the small town anyway. And now that she was gone, there was no reason for me to stay. It wasn't like I would want to hang around my parents since it was because of them and their goddamn lunacy that Lila had left.

With both of our fathers forbidding us to see each other, I could completely understand why Lila had run away from me. She didn't want to leave her life, her family, and her friends behind just to be with me. And she wasn't wrong to want that either.

As I sat there, thinking about all the things she and I had done and said to each other, I began to see a pattern. I'd been blind to the fact that I was a lot more like my father than I had realized.

From the first time I saw Lila, I'd wanted her. I'd gotten her in record time, too. I'd wanted to be with her as much as I possibly could. And I'd gotten that too.

The only thing I hadn't gotten was my father's blessing.

And maybe that was where things turned so dramatic. Maybe that was why we moved so fast with each other. Maybe the fact that our fathers had told us that the other person was off-limits had awoken the inner rebel in both of us.

Almost every moment we'd had was stolen. Every kiss we shared, forbidden. And when we'd made love, we'd broken all the rules.

After meeting that first night at my graduation party, we'd sped through the bases. First kiss was on night number one. Night number two, we rounded second base with extremely heavy petting. Morning number three, we made out in my truck just before the first specks of dawn, landing squarely on third base.

That same night, we slid into home plate when we made love in the back pasture of the ranch under the glow of a full moon and a blanket of stars. That was the first of many times we'd used that pasture and the night to hide us so that we could get as intimate as two people could possibly get.

We'd moved way too fast for a couple of virgins.

Better said, I moved way too fast.

Lila couldn't stop telling me how handsome I was and how she'd never touched muscles as big as mine. She would say how she wasn't anywhere near my league and that this had to be a dream.

I took advantage of her lust for me.

The one thing we knew for sure when we'd made those fast moves was that we weren't supposed to be together in the first place. And that there would be plenty to lose if we were ever discovered. Yet, we did it all anyway. And we continued doing it for another month.

Then I came up with the idea of getting married and moving away. I couldn't recall actually asking her to marry me, though. I did remember saying that I was going to make her my wife. But I never asked her to marry me.

I'm a goddamn fool!

Of course she'd gotten scared and ran away. Of course she felt bad about me being disowned and disinherited. Of course she'd asked to get out of town so that she didn't have to tell me to my face.

The only thing that didn't make sense was that she'd asked her father for help.

But at that point, I'd already manipulated her—even though I hadn't meant to—into having sex for the first time with a guy she'd only known for three days. And I continued rushing her when we got our marriage license and told her we'd get married in three days.

By that time, she was probably desperate enough to get away from me that she'd ask just about anyone for help. I was Mr. Three Days, after all. *Stupid! Stupid! Stupid!*

When you really love someone, you don't hurry things along.

At least, I guessed that's what you didn't do. I'd never been in love, so I had no idea how things were supposed to go. Maybe she had realized that.

Normal couples dated for a while, several months even before they moved on to having a sexual relationship. And then they dated—sometimes even for years—before the man asked his girl to marry him.

Not me, though. I went right for it. Sex—boom! Marriage—boom, boom!

I am such a moron.

Now I wished that I did have a party full of guys my age to hang out with and drown my sorrows. I needed some good male advice about women and the timeframe that went along with a good relationship.

But I hadn't even tried to get to know any of the guys at my party. Instead, I had focused all my attention on Lila. Like a freaking predator.

Lila was right to run off.

Her father had said that she didn't want to be the reason I lost everything. But that might've been the nicest way she knew how to say that she didn't want to see me anymore.

I knew that if she'd come to me and told me what she'd apparently told her father, I would've said that I didn't care if I lost everything. All that mattered was that I still had her.

After one month, I had the nerve to say something that fucking stupid.

Yet, even as I told myself how stupid that sounded, I couldn't help but feeling the same. I was only heartbroken that Lila didn't seem to feel that way as well. But if she had gone to so much trouble to ensure that I didn't throw away my future for us, then she must still care about me. Even if only a little bit.

Of course she did, she was that kind of girl. The kind who cared about everyone.

And she still deserved the world—even if she didn't want it

with me. She deserved to live at home, close to her friends and family. And she needed to know that I would leave her alone to live her life.

I owe her that much.

Reaching into the backseat, I grabbed my book bag. I'd write her a letter and get to the post office so it could go out first thing in the morning.

I wanted her to know that I would leave so that she could come back home and that I was as sorry as a person could be for what I'd done to her. And I wouldn't use the word love, not even once.

My hand shook as I held the pen at the top of the page, not knowing what the hell to say first.

Tossing the things into the passenger seat, I shouted, "Fuck it! I'll tell her in person."

23

LILA

My eyes flew open as I heard a familiar sound outside.

Coy's truck?

I had no idea how long I'd been sleeping or what time it was. It was dark in the room, which meant that it was still dark outside. The engine shut off, and then I heard a soft knock at the door.

Hilda had continued drinking wine, even after our long talk. I assumed she was passed out and couldn't hear the knocking on her front door. "Hilda," I shouted. "You have company."

More soft knocking came, but there were no other sounds. The knocking grew louder and more insistent. Then I heard Coy's voice. "Hilda, I know Lila is in there. Let me in. I just want to talk to her!"

Something crashed, and then I heard Hilda stumbling around. "No, no, no. This can't be happening."

"Coy!" I shouted.

Hilda was there in an instant, shoving a sock into my mouth, then wrapping a cord around my wrists to make sure that I couldn't get the sock out of my mouth. "Be quiet, or I'll shoot your little boyfriend."

I went still right away, not wanting anything bad to happen to Coy. He'd said that he knew I was in the house. I knew he wouldn't leave without seeing me for himself. I became very patient as I waited for things to play out.

The pounding never stopped. It seemed Coy wasn't about to give up. "Come on, Hilda. You've got to let me inside. I *have* to see her. I'll leave as soon as I tell her what I came here to say. I swear."

She looked at me with wide eyes. "You'd better be quiet."

I nodded and watched as she closed the door. I heard a sound as she slid something in front of it. She must've been making it look as if the door didn't exist.

Coy had to be smarter than Hilda if he was going to find me. But I knew he was smart. He could do it; I believed in him. So I stayed quiet. In my mind, though, I shouted to him that I was there.

The wooden floor creaked under Hilda's feet as she went from her bedroom to the front door. But I heard the sound of her cocking a shotgun, and my heart stopped. "You need to leave," she shouted. "I've got a shotgun—it's cocked and loaded. Unless you're bulletproof, I suggest you get back into your car and drive back to where you've come from."

"I can't go back until I've told her a couple things. Please, Hilda, let me in so I can set things straight with her. I'm begging you."

"I can't let you in," she told him.

"I won't tell a soul that you did it. And I'll give you any amount of money you want if you just let me in."

She was quiet for a long time. From the part of the house and the things in it that I could see, everything seemed to have been there for a very long time. The curtains, the blankets, and the sheets in the room I was in were so old that they were nearly see-through. It was obvious that she didn't have a lot of money.

I began moving my arms back and forth, trying to loosen up the cord she'd wrapped around my wrists. If I could get the damn sock out of my mouth, I could scream to alert Coy of my presence. And if he couldn't get inside to see me, he would call the cops.

Coy, please get help if you can't get inside this house!

"I can't do that. You need to leave." I could tell by the creaking floorboards that she'd slowly began moving closer to the door. If she got close enough, she could shoot him right through the door.

My heart sped up as panic spread through me like wildfire. Coy hadn't ever had to deal with something like this. I had no idea how much he even knew about guns and wooden doors and how easily the bullets could penetrate them. He might not even realize how vulnerable he was, standing on the other side, unaware of everything.

Aunt Hilda had not tied my feet. So I got out of the bed and kicked over the nightstand, making an enormous sound that brought Hilda running back to me.

A scraping sound told me she was moving whatever she'd put in front of the door, then it flew open, and she slapped me so hard that I stumbled back onto the bed.

Moving like lightning, she yanked the cord off the back of the little television and jumped onto the bed to sit on my legs. Holding them as still as she could as I kicked for all I was worth, she lashed the cord around my ankles, securely tying them up.

I'd never seen anything like it. And then I realized that I had. She'd used the same technique a cowboy used when he was tying up a calf's legs after roping it.

Hilda had some impressive skills, much to my dismay. I looked at her with wide eyes. Eyes that begged her to stop this insanity and to let Coy inside so that he could help me.

But she wouldn't look into my eyes as she left me again, closing the door and pushing something in front of it once more. She had no idea how much Coy and I loved each other—that was her biggest mistake.

Coy would never leave this place without seeing me. I knew

that for a fact. Hilda would've been better off answering the door and telling him that I wasn't there. But she'd chosen the wrong approach.

He knew I was there without a doubt now. Hilda's mistakes were paying off for me—big time. Coy knew I was inside this house. She'd made sure of that.

"What's going on in there?" Coy shouted. "You sound as if you're running all over the place. You don't need to be afraid. I'm not about to hurt you or anyone."

Hilda's voice sounded far away now; she must've been right at the front door. *"She's* running, Coy. She's trying to hide from you. She's afraid of you."

"Don't say that," he pleaded. "I'm sorry for what I've put her through. I want to apologize to her. I didn't realize I was rushing her—I didn't know that she might've felt I was manipulating her. It must be in my goddamn DNA. I don't know. But I have to apologize to her for scaring her—for making her feel that she had to run away."

I had no idea what he was talking about. *We* had gone that fast —not just him. I was part of everything we had done. I had wanted everything as much as him.

Why does he think he's manipulated me?

"She can hear you, so you have apologized. But she doesn't want to see you. I'm sorry. I'm her aunt. I have to do as she wishes," Hilda said. "And she doesn't want to see you, Coy. She's afraid of you."

My entire body froze with her lies. I wasn't afraid of Coy. I had never been afraid of him. I had no idea why he would think that, but he was wrong.

I loved Coy more than I'd loved anyone in my entire life. I was ready to leave my hometown for him. I was ready to leave my family for him. And I was ready to walk away from my friends for him too.

He can't believe her lies!

"I understand," came his weak response. He sounded as if he'd been stabbed directly in the heart.

And I felt the same way. *Please, God, don't let him leave me here.*

"Now go away, and don't come back," Hilda said.

"Hilda?" he asked with a voice full of tears.

"What?"

"Please let me in. I won't do anything to her or you. I've never been violent in my life, not even for one day. I'll give you every cent I have just to be able to see her."

With my eyes closed, I kept praying that my aunt would let Coy in. If he just got inside, then he would find me. I knew he would.

"If I let you in, you will have to understand that I can't let her go with you."

"Yeah, I know," he said.

"Okay. Give me a moment to get her ready. And be prepared to find her in a state that won't allow you to take her away. Okay?"

"Okay."

I couldn't believe it. She was going to let him in.

But she didn't come to set me free. She didn't move the barricade from in front of the door. She didn't do anything for such a long time that I wasn't even sure whether she was still awake.

Finally, Coy got impatient. "Hilda, what's going on in there?"

She walked in place, making it sound as if she was walking to the door from somewhere else. "Okay. I've got her ready. You do have money for me, right?"

"Yes, I have it in my hand. I'll give it to you as soon as you open the door."

"I have the shotgun. I'll use it on you if I have to."

"Yes, I know you will," he said with reverence.

I heard the locks clicking open as Hilda began unlocking the door. The squeak of the rusted hinges followed, and I couldn't believe that Coy was finally here to save me.

"You look look just like him," I heard her gasp. "Your father. Except for those eyes of yours."

"Apparently, I'm more like him than I knew. That's why I have to see Lila. I have to apologize for what I've done."

"You hurt her, didn't you?" she asked.

"I didn't mean to. But I must've hurt her for making her run away from everything—from me, her home, her town, her family and friends. I just want her to know that I'll accept the fact that she no longer wants to be with me, and then I'll leave Carthage so that she can get back to her life."

"That's incredibly sweet of you," Hilda said.

I started yelling behind my gag. I wanted to know why he thought all these things when none of them were true—but I knew he couldn't hear me.

"Who told you that she was here?" she asked.

"I'm not telling anyone that information. It doesn't matter anyway. I'm not going to try to change her mind. I just want to let her know that I'm incredibly sorry for what I've done."

"Don't be disturbed by what you see when I take you to her. I did this for her own good. And yours as well."

The sound of something being slid away from the door made my heart skip a beat. And then the door opened, and the light over the bed was turned on, nearly blinding me.

Coy gasped, and I blinked until I could see him. He had his hand over his mouth as he looked at me. I saw my aunt standing behind him with the gun aimed at his head.

With a sudden movement, he ducked and turned around fast, taking the shotgun away from her. She stumbled backward, as he'd slightly pushed her to get the gun. "No!"

Coy pointed the gun at her. "Unchain her right now, or I *will* kill you."

❧ 24 ❧

COY

I could not believe what I was seeing. Lila, with a chain around her body, hands and feet bound, and something shoved into her mouth. My stomach turned on itself as bile rushed up my throat.

How could she do this to her own flesh and blood?

Moving like the wind, I bent and bobbed as I turned to face Hilda, shoving her back. At the same time, I grabbed the barrel of the shotgun, jerking it out of her hands.

Cowering in front of me, she held up her hands. I wanted to shoot her for what she'd done to the woman I loved. But murder—even if justified—would put me in jail.

I have to stay free for Lila.

"Unchain her right now," I said sternly, "or I will *kill* you."

"Don't shoot me. I'll set her free. Just don't shoot me." Hilda moved like a serpent to get to the other side of the room. "The key to the padlock is in this drawer." She looked at me with worried eyes. "I've got to open it to get it out."

Lila's eyes stayed on me as I nodded. "If you pull anything other than the key out of there, I'm going to squeeze the trigger."

"Got it." She slowly opened the door, then pulled out the key.

Red filled my vision. I'd never been so angry in my entire life. The things this woman had done to Lila were horrifying. Lila had been gone three nights. I couldn't believe Lila had had to endure this torture for that long.

I wasn't about to let Hilda get a hold of anything sharp—and it would take something sharp to cut the electric cords that tied Lila's hands and feet. Glancing around the room, I saw a large pair of scissors on the floor in a corner.

After Hilda had unlocked the padlock that to the chain around Lila's waist, I said, "Put that chain around your waist now and use that padlock to close it. Then toss the key over here, to my feet."

Nodding, she did exactly as I'd said. Only then did I put the gun down near the door, out of Hilda's reach. I quickly moved to get the scissors, but before doing anything else, I took the thing out of Lila's mouth. "Coy, I'm so glad to see you!"

"I'm getting you out of here." I cut the cord binding her feet first. I looked at Hilda, who stood by the bed with her head hanging low— I needed to let her know that I wasn't going to let her get away with this. "I want you to tell me who asked you to do this to her."

"No one asked me to do this," Hilda lied.

"I know that's a lie!" My hand shook as I pointed the scissors at her. "Lila's father brought her to you. I already know that much. Now, tell me who orchestrated this entire thing. And tell me who told you to chain her up."

Hilda still wouldn't lift her head up to look at me. "Her father brought her to me. I was to chain her up only for one night. After that, I was supposed to let her out of the chains. But not until after I had talked some sense into her about staying away from you. I hadn't gotten that far yet. That's why she was still bound when you showed up."

"Tell me what role my father played in all of this." I was going to get to the bottom of this and make all of them pay dearly for what they'd done to Lila.

She finally lifted her head to look into my eyes. "Your father?"

I snipped the cord between Lila's wrists, setting her free. She immediately jumped into my arms and hugged me like she'd never let me go. "Coy! Thank God for you! I love you so much!"

"I love you too, baby." I used the blanket underneath her to cover her up as the rags she was wearing were barely covering her body. Turning my attention to Hilda, I said, "Yes, my father. Tell me how he was involved in all of this."

"I haven't spoken to your father since our high school days. This was all done by Lila's father. He wanted her to stay away from you. He'd forbidden her from seeing you, but she continued doing it anyway. So, he brought her to me. He wanted me to help make her accept the facts. Gentry men and Stevens women don't get to be together."

"Well, they do now." I didn't believe her for one second that she hadn't spoken to my father in years—I knew she was the person he'd spoken to on the phone. But my main concern was getting Lila the hell out of there. "I'm not sure what Lila and I are going to do about you and her father. She and I will make that decision together. You will never know whether the law is coming for you. Let that uneasiness rest solidly on your shoulders, Hilda Stevens. Kidnapping, false imprisonment, and torture can get you life in prison. Think long and hard about that."

I picked up the key to the padlock. Looking around, I wanted to be sure to place it somewhere she could get to and set herself free. But I wanted her to have to work for it.

There wasn't much in the room. But there was a dresser. I walked over to it, then lifted it up to examine how heavy it was. And it was very heavy. So, I leaned over and pushed the key underneath to make it extremely hard for her to reach.

"There you go. I've given you more than you ever gave Lila. And let me leave you with this. I hope you, and all who worked with you to do this to the woman I love, rot in hell for eternity. And may your life on Earth until your death be full of sorrow and hopelessness, because I am sure that's what Lila has been feeling since you people ripped her away from me."

A soft hand took mine, and I turned to find Lila shaking her head. "No, don't wish bad things on anyone. I'm okay, and you're okay, and that's what really matters."

She'd been the one who had gotten hurt, and yet here she was, telling me to leave the people who'd hurt her alone. "You're an angel. Do you know that?"

"Come on, babe. Let's just get out of here. I'm more than ready to move past this." She held my hand tightly, pulling me away to leave with her.

As we walked to the front door, I saw the cash I'd given Hilda lying on the coffee table. "I'm not about to let her keep this. Do you have anything else here that we need to get?" I picked up the several hundred dollars and put it into my pocket.

"No," she said as she pulled me to leave. "They took me out of my bed, tied me up, gagged me, and put a bag over my head before tossing me into the trunk of the car. I came with nothing more than the nightgown I'd had on."

I could not believe her own father had done that to her. There was absolutely nothing I could say to make things any better. But I would try to make her life happy until the day she died—if she'd allow me.

At one in the morning, Lila and I drove away from her aunt's house, heading toward Interstate 20. That would take us all the way to Dallas. I didn't want to take her anywhere near Carthage. Not yet.

"What were you talking about back there when you said that you'd manipulated me, Coy?" She pulled the ratty blanket around her shoulders a bit tighter, her eyes locked on mine.

"Well, I thought that you'd left town to get away from me. So, I thought about why you would've done that."

"Yeah, but I didn't leave you."

"I know that now."

"So why do you think you manipulated me?"

"I think that I pushed you without meaning to. I think I moved too fast. What do you think about the pace we've been moving at?"

She looked away from me, staring out the window as she fell quiet, presumably thinking about what I'd asked. When she looked back at me, she had a twinkle in her eyes. "Coy, I love you. I don't have a single regret about anything we've done in the short amount of time we've been together. We have moved fast, but we've continued moving forward with our relationship this whole time. I'm happy about us and our plans for the future. But if you're having doubts and want to wait, I'll understand."

"You don't want to wait to get married?" I thought I should rephrase that. "Wait a minute. I never asked you if you wanted to marry me in the first place. I just sort of told you that I wanted to marry you, didn't I? So, Lila, do you want to marry me?"

"I do." She smiled. "Do you want to marry me?"

"I do." I reached over and took her hand in mine, pulling her across the seat to sit right next to me. "How come you're sitting way over there when you can snuggle up against me?"

"I don't smell that good right now." She laughed as I tugged her. "Really, Coy. I stink. I haven't had a shower in three days."

Like I cared. "Get over here, girl." I pulled her to me, then draped my arm around her. "I don't care what you smell like. I just want to be able to hold you." It felt good to have her beside me again. "I'm gonna get us a hotel room in Dallas. After a shower and nap, we'll get up and go find a judge or Justice of the Peace to marry us. I brought our marriage license."

She sighed, and it sounded sad. "Coy, I'll need my driver's license to get married."

"You gave me your wallet. Don't you remember doing that?"

Perking up right away, she nodded. "Oh, yeah! This is great. We've got everything we need then."

"Are you sure that you're alright with making such a huge

decision right now?" She'd been through hell. "I don't want you to look back on this and have regrets."

"Coy, the truth is that I'll feel much safer with you as my husband." She placed her hand on my thigh, moving it back and forth. "With all that's happened to me, I feel as if I don't have a family anymore. You and I can be a family. We can make our own family."

"You want to start a family too?" I hadn't even thought about kids.

"If you do." She smiled coyly. "Why not start having kids right away? We've done everything else quickly. Why not get our family going too?"

"I don't know. I've got four years of college to get through. Plus, I'm pretty sure that I'll have to work for at least a little while. Dad will surely cut me off once I tell him that you and I are married. We should hold off trying to start our family until we know what our future holds."

"You're right. I guess we can take at least that one thing slow. Kids will come. I know that. But for now, I will be completely satisfied with being your wife."

I kissed her on the cheek. "I'm going to be more than satisfied by being your husband, Lila soon-to-be-Gentry."

"Wow," she whispered. "Lila Gentry. I bet your family never thought that a Gentry would marry a girl from the wrong side of town. Not even in a million years."

"We're gonna make some big changes in that little town we were born in. Just wait and see, Lila Gentry."

I meant that, too. Once I took over the ranch, things would be so different. And the Gentry name would be something my kids could be proud of—without their pride poisoning them into thinking that they were better than everyone else.

❧ 25 ❧

LILA

The next day, I sat in the truck next to my husband, wearing the white cotton dress he'd bought me. He wore a dark blue button-down shirt with black jeans and looked every bit as handsome as he had in the dream I'd had about marrying him.

With my left hand in his right one, I kept looking at the gold band he'd put on my finger only a few hours earlier. "I still can't believe we're married. This feels like a dream."

"It's not a dream. It's one hundred percent real." He pulled my hand up and kissed the ring. "You *are* my wife."

I laughed as that sounded crazy good to hear. "And you *are* my husband."

"I am that." He was driving out to the ranch to tell his family about our marriage. His plan was to tell them what had happened to me, hoping the insanity of my ordeal would help them change their minds about us.

It had never been my intention to get in the way of Coy and his inheritance or between him and his family. But he assured me that I wasn't in the way of anything. He said that if anyone was in the way of his happiness, it was his family, not me.

So, I sat there next to him with butterflies swarming inside my stomach. "I wonder if they'll accept us."

"You know, I'm still not sure about trusting my family just yet. I'm sure I heard my father talking to Hilda on the phone."

"We can't worry about that." I didn't want him to be angry at anyone over what had happened to me.

"Lila, I have to worry about that. If my family acts as if they accept this, then it might be a ploy to make us feel comfortable so you can be kidnapped again. And this time, they might take you even further away and make it harder—or even impossible—for me to find you."

"And you would call the police if that happened." I didn't think anyone would try to do such a thing to me again. They'd tried their best to stop us from being together, but now that we were married, nothing could separate us.

"I've just got this uneasy feeling. So, here's what we're going to do. We're going to tell my family about the marriage, and then we're going to tell them that we're moving right away to the house in Lubbock. I don't want us to spend even one night at the ranch."

"So, the plan is to let them know what we've done. Then, you'll get some of your things and pack them in the truck. After we'll go to my house where we'll tell my family, and I'll grab as many of my things as I can, and we'll be on our way to Lubbock?" It sounded like a lot of work and a lot of traveling. But how could I argue when he might be right not to trust any of them?

When we pulled into Carthage, he headed to the used car lot. "We'll pick up the car I bought for you before we do anything else. You can follow me out to the ranch. We'll leave the car at the gate just in case my father pulls some really shitty stuff with me."

"Like what?" I didn't know his father or what he was capable of. After talking to my aunt, I did have some vague ideas that he was into some rough stuff. But they were only ideas, not facts, so I kept them to myself.

"Hell, I don't know, Lila. I just don't want to risk losing everything we have. So we'll move everything that we have in the truck to the trunk of the car. And I mean everything. I'll even empty my pockets before we go and talk to them. I don't trust anyone but you at the moment."

"I hate things are this way." This was no way to start our lives together. I had to leave some hope in my heart that our families would see that we can't be stopped. There would be no reason to keep trying to keep us apart when we'd already gotten married.

After getting to the car, I got to work filling the trunk with Coy's bags, and then he took out his wallet and placed it there too. "That's it. That's everything we have, Lila. If everything goes to shit, we've got four-thousand dollars to our name."

I pointed out that we had more than that. "We've got the keys to the house in Lubbock as well, Coy. We will have a roof over our heads once we get there. And we'll also be stopping by my house to pick up some things." Suddenly, I realized that I didn't know much about the house in Lubbock. "Is the house furnished? Are there pots and pans, dishes, curtains, a television? You know, the stuff people use every day?"

"It's completely furnished with everything we'll need. All we really need to pack are our clothes and anything else that's personal. Everything else is there, waiting for us. There's even a washer and dryer from what my father told me."

"Cool." At least we would have the basics—that is, if Coy's father did take everything else away from him.

After closing the trunk, Coy and I stood there, looking at each other with rather grim expressions. He took me into his arms, holding me as he kissed the top of my head. "Change of plans. Let's go get your things before we go out to the ranch."

"Are you sure?" I had no idea how things would go with my family.

"Yeah. Leave the car here, and let's go in my truck. We'll

come back and put your things in the car, and then we'll head out to my place."

Although I felt uneasy, I got into the truck with him, and we went to my house. The car was gone, and that gave me some relief. "Looks like Dad might not be here. Come on, let's hurry." I'd packed most of my things in several bags in the closet before I'd gone to bed the night they took me away. It wouldn't take long for me to grab my things. Plus, I didn't have much in the first place.

Mom sat at the table as we walked through the door. Her eyes moved to Coy. "Hello." Then, she looked at me. "Lila! You're back home! I missed you so much." She got up, and I ran to hug her.

"Momma! It's so good to see you." I didn't want to let her go, but I knew we had to hurry before my father and brothers returned home.

Paul and Roman came running into the kitchen. "Lila!"

I let my mother go so that I could hug them both. "Boys!"

When I let them go, I saw Paul looking at Coy as he asked, "John? What's going on?"

"My name isn't John. I'm sorry that I lied to you, Paul. I'm Coy Gentry."

My mother sucked in her breath. "No!"

"Momma, it's okay. Coy rescued me. Dad took me to Aunt Hilda's."

"Yes, I know." She looked at me, confused. "But he did it because you asked him to. I called your aunt each day you were gone, and she told me that you were resting." My mother sat down hard in the chair. "What's going on?"

"Mom, I don't have much time. We need to leave before Dad and the boys get back. We don't want to make a scene, and I'm sure they'll cause one." I held out my hand to show her my ring. "Momma, we're married. I'm Lila Gentry now." I looked at my younger brothers. "Boys, can you grab the bags I have in the bottom of my closet and take them out to the truck? Coy and I are moving to Lubbock. He's got a house there. Once things settle down, I'll call you."

My brothers took off to get my things, and I followed to make sure we got everything. Coy came too, his hand in mine. "This is uncomfortable."

"Yeah, I know." I'd never felt so uncomfortable in my own home. But then again, I'd never been kidnapped by my own father either. "Let's get the hell out of here." I picked up the small suitcase with my makeup and hair products, then followed my brothers out to the truck.

"Don't wait too long to call us, Lila," Paul said. "I love you, sis."

"I love you both too. Be good for Momma." I felt a knot form in my throat and tried not to cry.

Getting into the truck, I gulped hard and grabbed my husband's hand as we left my family behind me. I felt as if it would be the last time I would be seeing them.

We drove in silence towards the car. Then, I got out of the truck and into it, following Coy to the ranch. Parking the car outside the entrance of the ranch, Coy and I began moving the things I'd gotten from my house into the car. The trunk and the backseat were now full of our things.

"There's not much room left," I said as I looked at everything.

"I don't have much left at home. I've already packed most of my things. What's left can fit in my truck. Dad gave me the truck for graduation. I don't really think he'll try to take it away from me. I mean, he might cut off my bank account for a while, but I don't expect him to do much more than that."

"But you never know," I said. "My father and aunt went to insane lengths to try and stop us from being together. And I'm still pretty sure your father was involved in some way or another. We have no idea what he'll do next."

Nodding, a frown formed on Coy's face as he took my hand

and led me to his truck. "Let's go see what kind of welcome we receive from my family, shall we?"

Biting my lip the whole way up the long, winding driveway, I felt like I might throw up. And as we parked the truck outside the side entrance, I felt like I might even pass out.

I clung to Coy as I walked beside him. "Coy, I'm so afraid."

"Don't be. We have each other, and that's all we will ever need. Everything else is just icing on the cake, baby."

Smiling, I didn't know how he was always able to make me feel better, but he had. "You're right."

We hadn't gotten to the door yet when his father stepped out. "What in the hell do you think you're doing, Coy Gentry?"

"I have something to tell you, Dad." Coy didn't bat an eye as he stood tall and faced his father. "Lila and I are married now. There's nothing anyone can do about it. And you should know that her own father kidnapped her, and she was chained up at her Aunt Hilda's house in Shreveport. For three days, this young woman was held captive by her own family. And I am here to ask you if you had anything to do with that."

I wasn't even aware that he was going to ask his father that. I'd thought we were going to give them the news of our marriage and see how they took it.

The sound of his mother's voice came from behind Coy's father, "He most certainly did not have anything to do with that, Coy. How dare you accuse your father of anything so heinous!"

Coy's eyes narrowed as he looked at his father. "I expect you to accept this marriage and to accept Lila as my wife and as part of this family. It will be our children who inherit this ranch someday."

"You think that you can shove this down my throat?" he asked with a grin. "You think that you can have what's mine to give?"

"I would like your blessing on my marriage," Coy said.

"No. You can't have that." Coy's father took a deep breath, his chest rising and falling, before he said, "You have a choice to make, son. You can get the marriage annulled and remain an eligible heir to Whisper Ranch. Or you can stay married and become a penniless son-of-a-bitch."

"Collin!" Mrs. Gentry gasped. "Don't do this."

"I won't have him doing this to our good name, Fiona. This is the way it has to be."

"Coy, please agree to the annulment. Don't give up everything for a girl you barely know," his mother begged.

I'd never seen the sheer determination that took over Coy's expression. "How long do you think you can go without seeing me?"

"Forever," his father said with no hesitation at all. "I will never be bullied by anyone. You will do as I say, or you can go to hell for all I care. So, is it an annulment?"

"I'm never leaving my wife. I love her, and I will never stop loving her. If you can't accept that, then you can go to hell." Coy's hand gripped mine so tightly that it hurt.

"Give me the keys to your truck," his father said. "You can leave this ranch with the clothes on your back, but nothing more than that. I'll have the bank account closed in minutes, and you can kiss the house in Lubbock goodbye as well as your college education. I won't be paying for any of it. I can sell that house back to the realtor in a matter of minutes."

Coy let go of my hand and walked toward his father. "Mom, can you get me a pen and some paper before I leave this Godforsaken place forever?"

"Coy, please listen to reason," she begged.

"Please, just do as I asked, Mom."

I had no idea what he was about to do as I stood there and waited, chewing my fingernails. Staring at the ground, I'd never been so nervous in my life.

Coy was giving up everything for me. He'd have nothing if we remained married. I wasn't sure I could take that kind of pressure.

When I looked back up, I saw Coy with the pen and paper. He placed the paper against the house's wall and then scribbled something on it. "Lila, can you come here please?"

I walked on shaky legs to his side, and then I saw what he'd written on the paper. He was giving up everything. He'd written that he and I never want anything from his family. The note stated it all in plain words. He signed it and then handed me the pen to do the same. Which I did.

I handed him the pen and stepped back. "Are you sure about this?"

"I've never been so sure of anything in my life." He put the paper on the step and then placed the pen on top of it. "There you go. You've successfully lost your son. Congratulations to you both."

Coy draped his arm around my shoulders as we walked away from his family, his inheritance, his ranch, and his life as he'd known it.

Kissing the side of my head as we walked down the long driveway, he said with such sincerity that it made me cry, "I've never felt freer. Thank you for giving me this, baby. Thank you for loving me and marrying me. It won't be the life I had hoped it would be, but it will be full of love and devotion."

And he was right. We'd found our happily ever after.

And I wouldn't have changed a single thing.

EPILOGUE

COLLIN

October 1990 – Carthage, Texas – Whisper Ranch

Things were never the same after Coy left us. Fiona never laughed again after that awful day. I never saw another smile curve her lips, which had become thin from the perpetual firm line she kept them in.

She never blamed me for his leaving. She never blamed me for anything. Maybe that's because she rarely spoke more than a word or two at a time since he'd left.

Even though her legs and back had healed, Fiona never moved out of the bedroom on the ground floor. And I never entered that room.

The maid had found her that morning. Lying in bed, hands clasped over her heart, Fiona wasn't breathing. The maid shouted for me to come, and I hurried to the bedroom.

My wife didn't move when I called out her name; her eyes remained shut. When I touched her cheek, I found it cold. "Call for help."

Plenty of help came. Only no one can bring the dead back to life. The coroner said that he would have to do an autopsy to confirm the cause of death, but he was fairly certain that her heart had given out. And I agreed with him.

Fiona's heart had shattered into a billion pieces the day we lost our only child. It was a miracle that she lasted the two years that she had.

My father died three days after Fiona's passing. And while we were burying him, my mother suffered a fatal stroke at the graveside service.

I found myself utterly alone for the first time in my life. And for a short time, I walked the halls of the ranch house in a numb state, waiting for death to come and find me.

My loneliness grew and grew until I realized that there was someone to blame for all that I'd lost. So, I sent for her. I had her brought to the ranch where I'd built a room just for her.

I hadn't laid eyes on her in many years. And the first time I saw her again, she kneeled in the room I'd made for her in my home. Her head tucked into her chest, dark eyes on the floor in front of her. "You failed at the one task I gave you, slave."

"And for that I am truly sorry, Master."

"You certainly will be." I picked up the black whip I'd brought in from the horse barn. "I've lost everyone because of you."

"I am truly sorry, Master," her words came out strong. But by the time I would be finished finished with her, she would barely be able to muster a whisper.

"My heart wasn't enough for you, was it?" I pulled back my arm, letting the whip's end dangle behind me. "You had to make sure I lost more than that. So you let my son take the girl. You let him ruin his life and mine."

Crack!

With the one lash, I'd split the naked caramel-colored back down the middle. "One."

The blood that peppered the thin line made me think about death. "My wife is gone because her heart could no longer take living without her son in her life." I pulled the whip back to ready myself to give her another lash. "For some reason, my father died, and then my mother died too. Within a week, I went from being a part of a family to being alone."

I let the whip fly and added another red stripe to her back. "Two."

"Now that I am all alone, you will serve to fill my time. I will use you any way I want. And I will punish you without mercy for what you've done to me." I gave her another red stripe on her bare back.

"Three." She sniffled as the blood ran down her back, pooling on the floor underneath her.

She'd had enough. But her pain—like mine—wouldn't end until we met our ends.

The pain began with us, and it would end with us. Only with my passing would Whisper Ranch become what it was meant to become.

Although my son would never see the ranch again, the heirs he gave me would someday call the place their own. They alone would fulfill the legacy their father had turned away from. They alone would have the opportunity to turn the ranch into something neither my father nor I ever could.

The future rests in the hands of those who have not yet been born. May God help them avoid the curse of being a man who carries the last name Gentry.

LILA

Present Day - Dallas, Texas

"I'm glad you saw my post on Facebook, Robert. It's been forever since I've been able to speak to you." I'd only recently gotten on social media to reconnect with family members I'd left behind in Carthage.

After leaving, Coy and I had made our way to Dallas, and that's where me made our home. We'd had three sons in that little house. But they'd left their father and me after Collin Gentry died. They had inherited Whisper Ranch and everything that went with it.

"Lila, it's so good to hear your voice. I can't recall the last time we spoke," my cousin said. "As soon as I read your post, talking about how your sons inherited their grandfather's ranch in Carthage and came into billions, I thought about my five nephews who lost their parents when they were kids."

"I heard about your brother and sister-in-law, Robert. Dying in a house fire is a tragic way to go. I can't imagine how those boys dealt with all that loss." My heart hurt for those kids, who had grown into men since losing their parents.

"Despite their bad luck, the boys have grown into good men. They all work hard, too. And they're as smart as can be. When I saw that your sons want to invest some of the money they've inherited to help their relatives make something out of themselves, I knew my nephews would be grateful for their help."

"What are they doing for work now?" I hoped things would work out for all of them.

"They're all in the hospitality industry, and one of them is a chef. They've talked about opening their own hotel or resort or something. But they don't have the credit to get the loans they would need to get things rolling. Maybe you could set up a meeting between them and your sons."

"I tell you what, why don't you talk to your nephews to find out if they have any worthwhile ideas, and then I'll relay that information to my sons?" I knew there would be many long-lost relatives who would want money from my boys. I was ready to weed out the good from the bad.

"Sure, I'll get back to you soon, Lila. And it was great hearing from you—even if you're not in love with the boys' ideas."

"I'm glad to hear you say that. I'd love it if we could all be close again. Now that my father has passed away, I finally feel like I can be around my family again. I look forward to hearing from you, Robert. God bless."

Coy came up behind me, wrapping his strong arms around me and kissing my cheek. "Sounds like you're already getting some nibbles. I'm glad our sons will start meeting some of their family members. And I'm happy they're going to help some of them get started with their own businesses. We raised great kids—even if we didn't have lots of money."

"The Nash brothers from Houston might be the first ones our sons help out." Turning in his arms, I wrapped my hands around him, then kissed him softly. "I'm proud of us, Coy. Damn proud."

The End of the Beginning –

Lightning Source UK Ltd.
Milton Keynes UK
UKHW022121220822
407683UK00011B/217